DOTTY DIMPLE'S FLYAWAY

SOPHIE MAY

Edition : Culturea (Hérault, 34)
Contact : infos@culturea.fr
Print in Germany by Books on Demand
Design and layout : Derek Murphy
Layout : Reedsy (https://reedsy.com/)
ISBN : 9791041819201
Légal deposit : July 2023

DOTTY DIMPLE'S FLYAWAY.

CHAPTER I.

BEGINNING TO REMEMBER.

Katie Clifford was a very bright child. She almost knew enough to keep out of fire and water, but not quite. She looked like other little girls, only so wise,—O, so very wise!—that you couldn't tell her any news about the earth, or the sun, moon, and stars, for she knew all about it "byfore."

Her hair was soft and flying like corn-silk, and when the wind took it you would think it meant to blow it off like a dandelion top. She was so light and breezy, and so little for her age, that her father said "they must put a cent in her pocket to keep her from flying away;" so, after that, the family began to call her Flyaway. She thought it was her name, and that when people said "Katie," it was a gentle way they had of scolding.

Everybody petted her. Her brother Horace put his heart right under her feet, and she danced over it. Her "uncle Eddard" said "she drove round the world in a little chariot, and all her friends were harnessed to it, only they didn't know it."

Her shoulders were very little, but they bore a crushing weight of care. From the time she began to talk, she took upon herself the burden of the whole family. When Mrs. Clifford had a headache, Flyaway was so full of pity that nothing could keep her from climbing upon the sufferer, stroking her face, and saying, "O, my dee mamma," or perhaps breaking the camphor bottle over her nose.

She sat at table in a high chair beside her father, and might have learned good manners if it had not been for the care she felt of Horace. She could scarcely attend to her own little knife and fork, because she was so busy watching her brother. She wished to see for herself that he was sitting straight, and not leaning his elbows on the table. If he made any mistake she cried, "Hollis!" in a tone as sweet as a wind-harp, though she meant it to be terribly severe, adding to the effect by shaking the corn-silk on her head in high displeasure. If she could correct him she thought she had done as much good in the family as if she had behaved well herself. He received all rebukes very meekly, with a "Thank you, little Topknot. What would be done here without you to preserve order?"

Flyaway could remember as far back as the beginning of the world,—that is to say, she could remember when her world began.

It is strange to think of, but the first thing she really knew for a certainty, she was standing in a yellow chair, in her grandmother Parlin's kitchen! It was as if she had always been asleep till that minute. People did say she had once been a baby, but she could not recollect that, "it was so many years ago."

Her mind, you see, had always been as soft as a bag of feathers; and nothing that she did, or that any one else did, made much impression. But now something remarkable was taking place, and she would never forget it.

It was this: she was grinding coffee. How prettily it pattered down on the floor! What did it look like? O, like snuff, that people sneezed with. This was housework. Next thing they would ask her to wash dishes and set the table. She would grow larger and larger, and Gracie would grow littler and littler; and O, how nice it would be when she could do all the work, and Gracie had to sit in mamma's lap and be rocked!

"Flywer'll do some help," said she. "Flywer'll take 'are of g'amma's things."

While she stood musing thus, with a dreamy smile, and turning the handle of the mill as fast as it would go round, somebody sprang at her very unexpectedly. It was Ruth, the kitchen-girl. She seized Katie by the shoulders, carried her through the air, and set her on her feet in the sink.

"There, little Mischief," said she, "you'll stay there one while! We'll see if we can't put a stop to this coffee-grinding! Why, you're enough to wear out the patience of Job!"

Katie had often heard about Job; she supposed it was something dreadful, like a lion, or a whale. She looked up at Ruth, and saw her black eyes flashing and the rosy color trembling in her cheeks. Cruel Ruth! She did not know Katie was her best friend, working and helping get dinner as fast as she could. "Ruthie," sobbed she, "you didn't ask please."

"Well, well, child, I'm in a hurry; and when you set things to flying, you're enough to wear out the patience of Job."

Job again.

"You've said so two times, Ruthie! Now I don't like you tall, tenny rate."

This was as harsh language as Katie dared use; but she frowned fearfully, and a tuft of hair, rising from her head like a waterspout, made her look so fierce that Ruth seemed to be frightened, and ran away with her apron up to her face.

The sink was so high that Katie could not get out of it alone,—"course indeed she couldn't."

"It most makes me 'fraid," said she to herself: "Ruthie's a big woman, I's a little woman. When I's the biggest I'll put Ruthie in my sink."

Very much comforted by this resolve, she dried her eyes and began to look about her for more housework. "Let's me see; I'll pump a bushel o' water."

There was a pail in the sink; so, what should she do but jump into that, and then jerk the pump-handle up and down, till a fine stream poured out and sprinkled her all over!

"Sing a song, O sink-spout," sang she, catching her breath: but presently she began to feel cold.

"O, how it makes me shivvle!" said she.

"Katie!" called out a voice.

"Here me are!" gurgled the little one, her mouth under the pump-nose.

When Horace came in she was standing in water up to the tops of her long white stockings. He took her out, wrung her a little, and set her on a shelf in the pantry to dry.

"Oho!" said she, shaking her wet plumage, like a duckling; "what for you look that way to me? I didn't do nuffin,—not the leastest nuffin! The water kep' a comin' and a comin'."

"Yes, you little naughty girl, and you kept pumping and pumping."

"I'm isn't little naughty goorl," thought Katie, indignantly; "but Ruthie's naughty goorl, and Hollis velly naughty goorl."

"O, here you are, you little Hop-o'-my-thumb," said Mrs. Clifford, coming into the pantry; "a baby with a cough in her throat and pills in her pocket musn't get wet."

Flyaway thrust her hand into her wet pocket to make sure the wee vial of white dots was still there.

"I fished her out of a pail of water," said Horace; "to-morrow I shall find her in a bird's nest."

Mrs. Clifford sent for some fresh stockings and shoes. Her baby-daughter was so often falling into mischief that she thought very little about it. She did not know this was a remarkable occasion, and the baby had to-day begun to remember. She did not know that if Flyaway should live to be an old lady, she would sometimes say to her grandchildren,—

"The very first thing I have any recollection of, dears, is grinding coffee in your great-grandmamma's kitchen at Willowbrook. The girl, Ruth Dillon, took me up by the shoulders, carried me through the air, and set me in the sink, and then I pumped water over myself."

This is about the way little Flyaway would be likely to talk, sixty years from now, adding, as she polished her spectacles,—

"And after that, children, things went into a mist, and I don't remember anything else that happened for some time."

Why was it that things "went into a mist"? Why didn't she keep on remembering every day? I don't know.

But the next thing that really did happen to Miss Thistleblow Flyaway, though she went right off and forgot it, was this: She persuaded her mother to write a letter for her to "Dotty Dimpwill." As it was her first letter, I will copy it.

"My dear Dotty Dimpwill first, then My Prudy:

"I'm going to say that I dink milk, and that girl lost my pills.

"I see a hop-toad. He hopped. Jennie took her up in his dress.

"And 'bout we put hop-toad in wash-dish. He put his foots out, stwetched, honest! He was a slippy fellow. First thing we knowed it, he hopped on to her dress. Isn't that funny?

"Now 'bout the chickens; they are trottin' round on the grass: they didn't be dead. We haven't got any only but dead ones; but Mis' Gray has.

"I like Dr. Gray ever so much!

"Mis' Gray gave me the kitty to play with. I bundled it all up in my dress, 'cause I didn't want the cat to get it. When I went home I gave it to the cat. [You got that wroten?]

"There wasn't any dead little kittens. She gave me a cookie, and I eated it, and I told her to give me another to bring home, 'cause I liked her cookies; they was curly cookies. [Got it wroted, mamma?]

"Now 'bout I pumped full a pail full o' water.

"[She knows we've got a house?]

"Now say good by, and I kiss her a pretty little kiss. O, no; I want her to come and see me,—her and Prudy,—two of 'em! I's here yet. ['Haps she knows it!]

"That's all—I feel sleepy.

(Signed) "From

"Dotty Dimpwill to Flywer."

This letter "went into a mist," and so did the next performance, which you will read in the following chapter.

CHAPTER II.

RUNNING AWAY TO CHURCH.

The little Parlins came the next week. One Sunday morning Dotty Dimple stood before the glass, putting on her hat for church. Katie came and peeped in with her, opening her small mouth and drawing her lips over her teeth, as her grandfather did when he shaved.

"See, Flyaway, you haven't any dimples at all!" said Dotty, primping a little. "Your hair isn't smooth and curly like mine; it sticks up all over your head, like a little fan."

"O, my shole!" sighed Flyaway, scowling at herself. She did not know how lovely she was, nor how

"The light of the heaven she came from
Still lingered and gleamed in her hair."

"I wisht 'twouldn't get out," said she.

"What do you mean by out?"

"O, unwetted, and un-comb-bid, and un-parted."

"That's because you fly about like such a little witch."

"I doesn't do the leastest nuffin, Dotty Dimpwill! Folks ought to let me to go to churches."

"I should laugh, Fly Clifford, to see you going to churches! All the ministers would come down out of the pulpits and ask what little mischief that was, and make aunt 'Ria carry you home!"

"No, he wouldn't, too! I'd sit stiller'n two, free, five hundred mouses," pleaded Flyaway, climbing up the back of a chair to show how quiet she could be.

"O, it's no use to talk about it, darling. Give me one kiss, and I'll go get my sun-shade."

"Can't, Dotty Dimpwill! My mamma's kiss I'll keep; it's ahind my mouf; she's gone to 'Dusty.

"Well, 'keep it ahind your mouf,' then; and here's another to put with it. What do you s'pose makes me love to kiss you so?"

"O, 'cause I so sweet," replied Flyaway, promptly; but she was not thinking of her own sweetness, just then; she was wondering if she could manage to run away to church.

"I'se a-goin' there myse'f! Sit still's a—a—" She looked around for a comparison, and saw a grasshopper on the window-sill: "still's a gas-papa. Man won't say nuffin' to me, see 'f he does!"

Strange such an innocent-looking child could be so sly! She ran down the path with Horace, kissing her little hand to everybody for good by, all the while thinking how she could steal off to church without being seen.

"You may go up stairs and lie down with me on my bed," said grandma, who was not very well. So Katie climbed upon the bed.

"My dee gamma, I so solly you's sick!" said she, stroking Mrs. Parlin's face, and picking open her eyelids. But after patting and "pooring" the dear lady for some time, she thought she had made her "all well," and then was anxious to get away. Mrs. Parlin wished to keep her up stairs as long as possible, because Ruth had a toothache.

"Shan't I tell you a story, dear?" said she.

"Yes, um; tell 'bout a long baby—no, a long story 'bout a short baby."

"Well, once there was a king, and he had a daughter—"

"O, no, gamma, not that! Tell me 'bout baby that didn't be on the bul-yushes; I don't want to hear 'bout Mosey!"

Grandma smiled, and wondered if people, in the good old Bible days, were in the habit of using pet names, and if Pharaoh's daughter ever called the Hebrew boy "Mosey." She was about to begin another story, when Flyaway said, "Guess I'll go out, now," and slid off the bed. There was an orange on the table. She took it, held it behind her, and walked quickly to the door. Looking back, she saw that her grandmother was watching her.

"What you looking at, gamma? 'Cause I'm are goin' to bring the ollinge right back."

And so she did, but not because it was wrong to keep it. Flyaway had no conscience, or, if she had any, it was very small, folded up out of sight, like a leaf-bud on a tree in the spring.

"Ask Ruthie to wash your face and hands, and then come right back to grandma and hear the story."

"Yes um."

Down stairs she pattered. The moment Ruth had kissed her, and turned away to make a poultice, she crept into the nursery, and put on Horace's straw hat. Then she took from a corner an old cane of her grandfather's, and from the paper-rack a daily newspaper, and started out in great glee. The "Journal" she hugged to her heart, and her short dress she held up to her waist, "'Cause I s'pect I mus' keep it out o' the mud," said she, as anxiously as any lady with a train.

She had no trouble in finding the church, for the road was straight, but the cane kept tripping her up.

"Naughty fing! Wisht I hadn't took you, to-day, you act so bad!" said she, picking herself up for the fifth time, and slinging the "naughty fing" across her shoulder like a gun. When she came to the meeting-house there was not a soul to be seen. "Guess they's eatin' dinner in here," decided Flyaway, after looking about for a few seconds. "Guess I'll go up chamer, see where the folks is."

Running away to Church.

Up stairs she clattered, hitting the balusters with her cane. Good Mr. Lee was preaching from the text, "Remember the Sabbath day, to keep it holy," and people could not imagine who was naughty enough to make such a noise outside—thump, thump, thump.

"Who's that a-talkin'?" thought Flyaway, startled by Mr. Lee's voice. "O, ho! that's the prayer-man a-talkin'. He makes me kind o' 'fraid!"

But just at that minute she had reached the top of the stairs, and was standing in the doorway.

"O, my shole! so many folks!"

She trembled, and was about to run away with her newspaper and cane; but her eyes, in roving wildly about, fell upon grandpa Parlin and all the rest of them, in a pew very near the pulpit. Then she thought it must be all right, and, taking courage, she marched slowly up the aisle, swinging the cane right and left.

Everybody looked up in surprise as the droll little figure crept by. Grandpa frowned through his spectacles, and aunt Louise shook her head; but Horace hid his face in a hymn-book and Dotty Dimple actually smiled

"They didn't know I was a-comin'," thought Flyaway, "but I camed!"

And with that she fluttered into the pew.

"Naughty, naughty girl," said aunt Louise, in an awful whisper.

She longed to take up the morsel of naughtiness, called Katie, in her thumb and finger, shake it, and carry it out. But there was a twinkle in the little one's eye that might mean mischief; she did not dare touch her.

"O, what a child!" said aunt Louise, taking off the big hat and setting Flyaway down on the seat as hard as she could.

Flyaway looked up, through her veil of flossy hair, at her pretty auntie with the roses round her face.

"Nobody didn't take 'are o' me to my house," said she, in a loud whisper, "and that's what is it!"

"Hush!" said aunt Louise, giving Flyaway another shake, which frightened her so that she dropped her head on her brother's shoulder, and sat perfectly still for half a minute.

Aunt Louise was sadly mortified, and so were Susy and Prudy. They dared not look up, for they thought everybody was gazing straight at the Parlin pew, and laughing at their crazy little relative. Horace and Dotty Dimple did not care in the least; they thought it very funny.

"They shan't scold at my cunning little Topknot," whispered Horace, consolingly. "Sit still, darling, and when we get home I'll give you a cent."

"Yes um, I will," replied poor brow-beaten Flyaway, and held up her head again with the best of them. Perhaps she had been naughty; perhaps folks were going to snip her fingers; but "Hollis" was on her side now and forever. She began to feel quite contented. She had got inside the church at last, and was very well pleased with it. It was even queerer than she had expected.

"What was that high-up thing the prayer-man was a-standin' on?"

Flyaway merely asked this of her own wise little brain. She concluded it must be "a chimley."

"Great red curtains ahind him," added she, still conversing with her own little brain. "Lots o' great big bubbles on the walls all round. Big's a tea-kiddle! Lamps, I s'pose. There's that table. Where's the cups and saucers for the supper? And the tea-pot?

"All the bodies everywhere had their bonnets on; why for? Didn't say a word, and the prayer-man kep' a-talkin' all the time; why for? Flywer didn't talk; no indeed. Folks mus'n't. If folks did, then the man would come down out the chimley and tell the other bodies to carry 'em home. 'Cause it's the holy Sabber-day,—and that's what is it."

Flyaway's airy brain went dancing round and round. She slid away from Horace's shoulder, spread her little length upon the seat, closed her wondering, tired eyes, and sailed off to Noddle's Island. A fly, buzzing in from out doors, had long been trying to settle on Flyaway's restless nose. He never did settle: Horace kept guard with a palm-leaf fan, and "all the other bodies" in the pew sat as still as if they had been nailed down; so anxious were they to keep the little sleeper safely harbored at Noddle's Island.

"Such a relief!" thought aunt Louise, venturing to look up once more.

Flyaway did not waken till the last prayer, when Horace held her fast, lest she should make a sudden rush upon a speckled dog, which came trotting up the aisle.

On the steps they met Ruth, with wild eyes and face tied up in a scarf, hunting for Flyaway. Mrs. Parlin, she said, was going up the hill, so frightened that it would make her "down sick."

When grandma got home, all out of breath, she found Flyaway looking very downcast. Her heart was heavy under so many scoldings. "O, Katie," said grandma, "how could you run away?"

"I didn't yun away," replied Flyaway, thrusting her finger into her mouth; "I walked away!"

"There, if that isn't a cunning baby, where'll you find one?" whispered brother Horace to Prudy. "Grandmother can't punish her after such a 'cute speech."

But grandmother could, and did. She took her by the little soft hand, led her to the china closet, and locked her in.

"Half an hour you must stay there," said she, "and think what a naughty girl you've been!"

"Yes um," said Flyaway, meekly, and wiped off a tear with the hem of her frock.

But the moment she was left alone, her quick, observing eyes saw something which gave her a thrill of delight. It was a jar of quince jelly, which had been left by accident on the lower shelf.

"'Cause I spect I likes um," said she, serenely, after eating all she possibly could.

At the end of half an hour grandma came and turned the key.

"Have you been thinking, dear, and are you sorry and ready to come out?"

"Yes, um," replied the little culprit, with her mouth full, and feeling very brave as long as the door was shut between her and her jailer. 'Yes, um, I've thought it all up,—defful solly. But you won't never shut me up no more, gamma Parlin!"

"Katie Clifford!" said grandma, sternly; and then she opened the door, and faced Flyaway.

"'Cause—'cause—'cause," cried the little one, in great alarm; "you won't shut me up, 'cause I won't never walk away no more, gamma Parlin!"

Mrs. Parlin tried hard not to smile; but the mixture on Flyaway's little face of naughtiness, jelly, and fright, was very funny to see.

The child noticed that her grandmother's brows knit as if in displeasure, and then she remembered the jelly.

"I hasn't been a-touchin' your 'serves, gamma," said she.

Mrs. Parlin really did not know what to do,—Flyaway's conscience was so little and folded away in so many thicknesses, like a tiny pearl in a whole box of cotton wool. How could anybody get at it?

"Gamma, I hasn't been a-touchin' your 'serves," repeated the little thief.

"Ah, don't tell me that," said grandma, sadly; "I see it in your eye!"

"What, gamma, the 'serves in my eye?" said Flyaway, putting up her finger to find out for herself. "'Cause I put 'em in my mouf, I did."

Mrs. Parlin washed the little pilferer's face and hands, took her in her lap, and tried to feel her way through the cotton wool to the tiny conscience.

The child looked up and listened to all the good words, and when they had been spoken over and over, this was what she said:—

"O, gamma, you's got such pitty little wrinkles!"

CHAPTER III.

RUNNING AWAY TO HEAVEN.

About ten o'clock one morning, Flyaway was sitting in the little green chamber with Dotty Dimple and Jennie Vance, bathing her doll's feet in a glass of water. Dinah had a dreadful headache, and her forehead was bandaged with a red ribbon.

"Does you feel any better?" asked Flyaway, tenderly, from time to time; but Dinah had such a habit of never answering, that it was of no use to ask her any questions.

Dotty Dimple and Jennie were talking very earnestly.

"I do wish I did know where Charlie Gray is!" said Dotty, looking through the open window at a bird flying far aloft into the blue sky.

"You do know," answered Jennie, quickly; "he's in heaven."

"Yes, of course; but so high up—O, so high up," sighed Dotty, 'it makes you dizzy to think."

"Can um see we?" struck in little Flyaway, holding to Dinah's flat nose a bottle of reviving soap suds.

"Prudy says it's beautiful to be dead," added Dotty, without heeding the question; "beautiful to be dead."

"Shtop!" cried Flyaway; "I's a-talkin'. Does um see we?"

"O, I don' know, Fly Clifford; you'll have to ask the minister."

Flyaway squeezed the water from Dinah's ragged feet, and dropped her under the table, headache and all. Then she tipped over the goblet, and flew to the window.

"The Charlie boy likes canny seeds; I'll send him some," said she, pinning a paper of sugared spices to the window curtain, and drawing it up by means of the tassel. "O, dear, um don't go high enough. Charlie won't get 'em "

"Why, what is that baby trying to do?" said Dotty Dimple.

"Charlie's defful high up," murmured Flyaway, heaving a little sigh; "can't get the canny seeds."

"O, what a Fly! How big do you s'pose her mind is, Jennie Vance?"

"Big as a thimble, perhaps," replied Jennie, doubtfully.

"Why, I shouldn't think, now, 'twas any larger than the head of a pin," said Dotty, with decision; "s'poses heaven is top o' this room! Why, Jennie Vance, I persume it's ever so much further off 'n Mount Blue—don't you?"

"O, yes, indeed! What queer ideas such children do have! Flyaway doesn't understand but very little we say, Dotty Dimple; not but very little."

Flyaway turned round with one of her wise looks. She thought she did understand; at any rate she was catching every word, and stowing it away in her little bit of a brain for safe keeping. Heaven was on Mount Blue. She had learned so much.

"But I knowed it by-fore," said she to herself, with a proud toss of the silky plume on the crown of her head.

"Shall we take her with us?" asked Jennie Vance.

Flyaway listened eagerly; she thought they were still talking of heaven, when in truth Jennie only meant a concert which was to be given that afternoon at the vestry.

"Take that little snip of a child!" replied Dotty; "O, no; she isn't big enough; 'twouldn't be any use to pay money for her!"

With which very cutting remark Dotty swept out of the room, in her queenly way, followed by Jennie. Flyaway threw herself across a pillow, and moaned,—

"O, dee, dee!"

Her little heart was ready to bleed; and this wasn't the first time, either. Those great big girls were always running away from her, and calling her "goosies" and "snips;" and now they meant to climb to heaven, where Charlie was, and leave her behind.

"But I won't stay down here in this place; I'll go to heaven too, now, cerdily!" She sprang from the pillow and stood on one foot, like a strong-minded little robin that will not be trifled with by a worm. "I'll go too, now, cerdily."

Having made up her mind, she hurried as fast as she could, and tucked a stick of candy in her pocket, also the bottle of soap suds, and two thirds of a "curly cookie" shaped like a leaf. "Charlie would be so glad to see Fly-wer!" She purred like a contented kitten as she thought about it. "'Haps they've got a bossy-cat up there, and a piggy, and a swing. O, my shole!"

There was no time to be lost. Flyaway must overtake the girls, and, if possible, get to heaven before they did. She flew about like a distracted butterfly.

"I must have some skipt; her said me's too little to pay for money;" and she curled her pretty red lip; "but I'm isn't much little; man'll want some skipt."

For she fancied somebody standing at the door of heaven holding out his hand like the ticket-man at the depot. She found her mother's purse in the writing-desk, and scattered its contents into the wash-bowl, then picked out the wettest "skipt," a five-dollar bill, and tucked it into her bosom. This would make it all right at the door of heaven.

"Now my spetty-curls," she added, hunting in the "uppest drawer" till she found the eyeless spectacles used for playing "old lady." With these on, Flyaway thought she could see the way a great deal better. Horace's boots would help her up hill; so she jumped into those, and clattered down the back stairs with Dinah under her arm.

There was nobody in the kitchen, for Ruthie was down cellar sweeping. Flyaway caught her shaker off the "short nail," and stole out without being seen. Sitting in the sun on the piazza was the "blue" kittie. "Finkin' bout a mouse, I spect," said little Flyaway, seizing her and blowing open her eyes like a couple of rosebuds.

"Does you know where I's a-goin'? Up to heaven. We don't let tinty folks, like cats, go to heaven."

Pussy winked sorrowfully at this, and baby's tender heart was touched.

"Yes, we does," said she; "but you musn't scwatch the Charlie boy;' and she tucked the "tinty folks" under her left arm. Then all was ready, and the little pilgrim started for heaven.

"Um's on the toppest hill," said she, looking at the far-off mountains, reaching up against the blue sky. One mountain was much higher than the others, and on that she fixed her eye. It was Mount Blue, and was really twenty miles away. If Flyaway should ever reach that cloud-capped peak, it was not her wee, wee feet which would carry her there. But the baby had no idea of distances. She went out of the yard as fast as the big boots would allow. She felt as brave as a little fly trying to walk the whole length of the Chinese Wall.

Where were Dotty Dimple and Jennie Vance? O, they were half way to heaven by this time; she must "hurry quick."

The fact was, they were "up in the Pines," picking strawberries. Nobody saw Flyaway but a caterpillar.

"O, my shole! there's a catty-pillow—what he want, you fink?"

Kitty winked and Dinah sulked, but there was no reply.

The next thing they met was a grasshopper. "O, dee, a gas-papa! Where you s'pose um goin'?"

Kitty winked again and Dinah sulked.

Flyaway answered her own question. "Diny, dat worm gone see his mamma."

Dinah did not care anything about the family feelings of the "worms;" so she kept her red silk mouth shut; but she grew very heavy—so heavy indeed, that once her little mother dropped her in the sand, but picking her up, shook her and trudged on. Presently she dropped something else, and this time it was the kitty. Flyaway turned about in dismay.

"Shtop," cried she, scowling through her "spetty-curls," as she saw three white paws and one blue one go tripping over the road. "Shtop!" But the paws kept on.

"O, Diny," said Flyaway, as pussy's tail disappeared round a corner,—"O, Diny, her don't want to go to heaven!"

Then Flyaway sat down in the sand, and pulled off one of the big boots.

"Um won't walk," said she; but, before she had time to pull off the second one, a dog came along and frightened her so she tried to run, though she only hopped on one foot, and dragged the other. She did not know what the matter was till she fell down and the boot came off of itself, after which she could walk very well. What cared she that both "Hollis's" new boots were left in the road, ready to be crushed by wagon wheels?

She kept on and kept on; but where was that blue hill going to? It moved faster than she did.

"Makes me povokin'," said she, giving Dinah a shake. "Um runs away and away, and all off!"

Sometimes she remembered she was going to heaven, and sometimes she forgot it. She was on the way to the "Pines," and many little flowers grew by the road-side. She began to pick a few, but the thorns on the raspberry bushes tore her tender hands, and one of the naughty branches caught Dinah by the frizzly hair, and carried her under. What did Flyaway spy behind the bushes? Dotty Dimple and Jennie Vance. They were eating wintergreen leaves; they did not see her. Flyaway kept as still as if she were sitting for a photograph, picked up Dinah, gave her a hug, and crept on.

She went so quietly that nobody heard her. When she was out of sight she purred for joy. She had got ahead of the girls on the way to heaven! She took the stick of candy out of her pocket and nibbled it to celebrate the occasion. "A little hump-backed bumblebee" saw her do it. He wanted some too, and followed Flyaway as if she had been a moving honeysuckle. For half a mile or more she "gaed" and she "gaed," all the while nibbling the candy; but now she was growing very tired, and did it to comfort herself. Suddenly she remembered it was Charlie's candy. She held it up to her tearful eyes.

"O dee," said she, "it was big, but it keeps a-gettin' little!"

The hungry bumblebee, who was just behind her, thought this was his last chance: so he pounced down upon Charlie's candy; and being cross, and not knowing Flyaway from any other little girl, he stung her on the thumb. Then how she cried, "'Orny 'ting me! 'Orny 'ting me!" for she had been treated just so before by a hornet. "O my dee mamma! My dee mamma!"

But her "dee" mamma could not hear her; she was in the city of Augusta; and as for the rest of the family, they supposed Flyaway was playing "catch" with Dotty Dimple in the barn.

CHAPTER IV.

"A RAILROAD SAVAGE."

It now occurred to little Flyaway, with a sudden pang, that she must have come to the end of the world. "Yes, cerdily!" The world was full of folks and houses,—this place was nothing but trees. The world had horses and wagons in it,—this place hadn't. "O dee!"

Where was the hill gone, on the top of which stood that big house they called heaven,—the house where Charlie lived and played in the garden? Why, that hill had just walked off, and the house too! She parted the bushes and peeped through. Nothing to be seen but trees. Flyaway began to cry from sheer fright, as well as pain. "'Tis a defful day! I can't stay in this day!"

More trouble had come to her than she knew how to bear; but worst of all was the cruel stab of the bumblebee. She pitied her aching "fum," and kissed it herself to make it feel better; but all in vain; "the pain kept on and on;" the "fum" grew big as fast as the candy had grown little.

"Somebody don't take 'are o' me," wailed she; "somebody gone off, lef' me alone!"

She was dreadfully hungry. "When was it be dinner time?" She would not have been in the least surprised, but very much pleased, if a bird had flown down with a plate of roast lamb in his bill, and set it on the ground before her. Simple little Flyaway! Or if her far-away mother had sprung out from behind a tree with a bed in her arms, the tired baby would have jumped into the bed and asked no questions.

But nothing of the sort came to pass. Here she was, without any heaven or any mother; and the great yellow sun was creeping fast down the sky.

"I'm tired out and sleepy out," wailed the young traveller, the tears rolling over the rims of her "spetty-curls,"—"all sleepy out; and I can't get rested 'thout—my—muvver!"

She sat down and hid her head in her black dolly's bosom.

"Diny, you got some ears? We wasn't here by-fore!"

This was all the way she had of saying she was lost.

The sky suddenly grew dark; a shower was coming up.

"Where has the bwight sun gone?" said Flyaway, with a shudder.

She was answered by a peal of thunder,—wagon-wheels, she supposed.

"Here I is!" shouted she.

Some one had come for her. Perhaps it was Charlie, and they meant to give her a ride up to heaven. A flash of light, and then another crash. Flyaway understood it then. It was logs. People were rolling logs up in the sky, on the blue floor. She had seen logs in a mill. Such a noise!

Then she dropped fast asleep, and somebody came right down out of the clouds and gave her a peach turnover as big as a dinner basket, or so she thought. Just as she was about to cut it, she was awakened by the rain dripping into her eyes. She started up, exclaiming, "If you pees um, I want some cheese um."

But the turnover had gone! Then the feeling of desolation swept over her again. She had come to the end of the world, and dinner, and mother, and heaven had all gone off and left her.

"O, Diny," sobbed she, turning to her unfeeling dolly for sympathy. 'I's free years old, and you's one years old. Don't you want to go to heaven, Diny, and sit in God's lap? What a great big lap he must have!"

A gust of wind lifted the frizzles on Dinah's forehead, but that was all.

"O dee, dee, dee! you don't hear nuffin 't all, Diny," said Flyaway—the only sensible remark she had made that day. It was of no use talking to Dinah; so she began to talk to herself.

"What you matter, Flywer Clifford?" said she, scowling to keep her courage up. "What you matter?"

And after she had said that, she cried harder than ever, and crept under the bushes, moaning like a wounded lamb.

"I'm defful wetter, but I'm colder'n I's wetter; makes me shivvle!"

After a while the clouds had poured out all the rain there was in them, and left the sky as clear as it was before; but by that time the sun had gone to bed, and the little birds too, sending out their good nights from tree to tree. Then the new moon came, and peeped over the shoulder of a hill at Flyaway. She sprang out from the bushes like a rabbit.

"O, my shole!' cried she, clapping her hands, "the sun's camed again! A little bit o' sun. I sawed it!"

Lost in the Woods.

Inspired with new courage, she and Dinah concluded to start for home; that is to say, they turned round three or four times, and then struck off into the woods.

Now you may be sure all this could not happen without causing great alarm at grandpa Parlin's. When the dinner bell rang, everybody asked, twice over, "Why, where is little Fly?" and Dotty Dimple answered, as innocently as if it were none of her affairs,—

"Why, isn't she in the house? We s'posed she was. Jennie Vance and I have just been out in the garden, under your little crying willow, making a wreath. Thought she was in the barn, or somewhere."

"But you haven't been in the garden all the while?"

"No'm; once we went up in the Pines,—grandma, you said we might,—but we haven't seen Fly,—why, we haven't seen her for the longest while!"

Grace had dropped her knife and fork and was looking pale.

"It was Susy and I that had the care of her, grandma; when you went out to see the sick lady, you charged us, and we forgot all about it."

"Pretty works, I should think!" cried Horace, springing out of his chair; "I wouldn't sell that baby for her weight in gold; but I reckon you would, Grace Clifford, and be glad of it, too."

Grandma held up a warning finger. "I declare," said aunt Louise, very much agitated, "I never shall consent to have Maria go out of town again, and leave Katie with us. If she will try to swim in the watering-trough, she is just as likely to take a walk on the ridgepole of the house."

Horace darted out of the room with a ghastly face, but came back looking relieved. He had been up in the attic, and climbed through the scuttle, without finding any human Fly on the roof, or on the dizzy tops of the chimneys, either.

But where was the child? Had Ruth seen her? Had Abner?

No; the last that could be remembered, she had been playing by herself in the green chamber, soaking Dinah's feet in a glass of water. The "blue kitty," the only creature who had anything to tell, sat washing her face on the kitchen hearth, and yawning sleepily. Fly's shaker was gone from the "short nail," and aunt Louise discovered some bank-bills in a wash-bowl,—"Fly's work, of course." But this was all they knew.

Grandpa searched the barn, Abner the fields, Ruth the cellar; aunt Louise and Horace ran down to the river. In half an hour several of the neighbors had joined in the search.

"I always thought there would be a last time," said poor Mrs. Dr. Gray, putting on her black bonnet, and joining Grace and Susy. "That child seems to me like a little spirit, or a fairy, and I never thought she would live long. She and Charlie were too lovely for this world."

"O, don't, Mrs. Gray," said Grace. "If you knew how often she'd been lost, you would not say so! We always find her, after a while, somewhere."

Horace, who had gone on in advance, now came running back, swinging his boots in the air.

"A trail!" cried he. "I've found a trail! Who planted these boots in the road, if it wasn't Fly Clifford?"

"Perhaps she has gone to aunt Martha's," said Mrs. Parlin, "or tried to. Strange we did not think of that!"

But aunt Martha had not seen her, nor had any one else. Horace and Abner went up to the Pines, but the forest beyond they never thought of exploring; it did not seem probable that such a small child could have strolled to such a distance as that.

Supper time came and went. There was a short thunder-shower. The Parlins shuddered at every flash of lightning, and shivered at every drop of rain; for where was delicate, lost little Fly?

Abner and Horace were out during the shower. Horace would have braved hurricanes and avalanches in the cause of his dear little Topknot.

"There's one thing we haven't thought of," said Abner, shaking the drops from his hat and looking up at the sky, which had cleared again; "we haven't thought of the railroad surveyors! They are round the town everywhere with their compasses and spy-glasses."

It was not a bad idea of Abner's. He and Horace went to the hotel where the railroad men boarded. The engineer's face lighted at once.

"I wish I had known before there was a child missing," he said. "I saw the figure of a little girl, through my glass, not an hour ago. It was a long way beyond the Pines, and I wondered how such a baby happened up there but I had so much else to think of that it passed out of my mind."

About eight o'clock, Flyaway was found in the woods, sound asleep, under a hemlock tree, her faithful Dinah hugged close to her heart.

There was a shout from a dozen mouths. Horace's eyes overflowed. He caught his beloved pet in his arms.

"O, little Topknot!" he cried. "Who's got you? Look up, look up, little Brown-brimmer."

All Flyaway could do was to sob gently, and then curl her head down on her brother's shoulder, saying, sleepily, "Cold, ou' doors stayin'."

"Why did our darling run away?"

"Didn't yun away; I's goin' up to heaven see Charlie," replied Flyaway, suddenly remembering the object of her journey, and gazing around at Abner, Dr. Gray, and the other people, with eyes full of wonder. "Where's the toppest hill? I's goin' up, carry Charlie some canny."

The people formed a line, and, as Prudy said, "processed" behind Katie all the way to the village.

"Is we goin' to heaven?" said the child, still bewildered. "It yunned away and away, and all off!"

"No, you blessed baby, you are not going to heaven just yet, if we can help it," answered Dr. Gray, leaning over Horace's shoulder to kiss the child.

Flyaway was too tired to ask any more questions. She let first one person carry her, and then another, sometimes holding up her swollen thumb, and murmuring, "'Orny 'ting me—tell my mamma." And after that she was asleep again.

Dotty Dimple, Susy, and Prudy were pacing the piazza when the party arrived, but poor grandma was on the sofa in the parlor, quite overcome with anxiety and fatigue, and Miss Polly Whiting was mournfully fanning her with a black feather fan. The sound of voices roused Mrs. Parlin. "Safe! safe!" was the cry. Dotty Dimple rushed in, shouting, "A railroad savage found her! a railroad savage found her!"

In another moment the runaway was in her grandmother's lap. All she could say was, "'Orny 'ting me on my fum! 'Orny 'ting me on my fum!" For this one little bite of a bee seemed greater to Flyaway Clifford than all the dangers she had passed. If grandma would only kiss her "fum," it was no matter about going to heaven, or even being undressed.

But after she had had a bowl of bread and milk, and been nicely bathed, she forgot her sufferings, and laughed in her sleep. She was dreaming how Charlie came to the door of heaven and helped her up the steps.

CHAPTER V.

EAST AGAIN.

A whole year passed. Dotty Dimple became a school-girl, with a "bosom friend" and a pearl ring. Prudy, who called herself "the middle-aged sister," grew tall and slender. Katie was four years old, and just a little heavier, so she no longer needed a cent in her pocket to keep her from blowing away.

The Parlins had been at Willowbrook a week before the Cliffords arrived. There was a great sensation over Katie. She was delighted to hear that she had grown more than any of the others.

"I'm gettin' old all over!" said she, gayly. "Four—goin' to be five! Wish I was most six. Dotty Dimpul, don't you wish you's most a hunderd?"

"O, you cunning little cousin!" said Dotty, embracing her rapturously; "I wish you loved me half as well as I love you; that's what I wish. I told Tate Penny you were prettier than Tid; and so you are. Such red cheeks! But what makes one cheek redder than the other?"

"O, I eat my bread 'n' milk that side o' my mouf," replied Flyaway; "and that's why."

"What an idea! And your hair is just as fine as ever it was; the color of my ring—isn't it, Prudy?"

Flyaway put her little hand to her head, and felt the floss flying about as usual.

"My hair comes all to pieces," explained she; "or nelse I have a ribbon to tie it up with."

"Are you glad to come back to Willowbrook, you precious little dear?" asked two or three voices.

"Yes 'm," said Flyaway, doubtfully; "Y—es—um."

"She doesn't remember anything about it, I guess," said Prudy, kneeling before the little one, and kissing the sweet place in her neck.

"Yes, I do," said Flyaway, winking hard and breathing quick in the effort to recall the very dim and very distant past; "yes, I 'member."

"Well, what do you 'member?"

"O, once I was grindin' coffee out there in a yellow chair, and somebody she came and put me in the sink."

"She does know—doesn't she?" said Dotty. "That was Ruthie; come out in the kitchen and see her."

But when Flyaway first looked into Ruth's smiling face, with its black eyes and sharp nose, she could not remember that she had ever seen it before. Abner, too, was strange to her.

"Come here," said he, "and I can tell in a minute if you are a good little girl."

Flyaway cast down her soft eyes, and sidled along to Abner.

"Here, touch this watch," said he, "and if you are a good little girl it will fly open; if you are naughty it will stay shut."

Flyaway looked askance at Abner, her finger in her mouth, but dared not touch the watch.

"Who'd 'a thought it, now?" said Abner, pretending to be shocked. "Looks to be a nice child; but of course she isn't, or she'd come right up and open the watch."

Flyaway thrust another finger in her mouth, and pressed her eyelids slowly together. Abner did not understand this, but it meant that he had not treated her with proper respect.

"Here, Ruth," said he, in a low tone, "hand me one of your plum tarts; that'll fetch her.—Come here, my pretty one, and see what's inside of this little pie."

Flyaway was very hungry. She took a step forward, and held her hand out, though rather timidly.

"But she mustn't eat it without asking her mamma," said Ruth.

"Yes; O, yes," cried Miss Flyaway, opening her little mouth for the first time, and shutting it again over a big bite of tart; "I want to eat it and s'prise my mamma."

Abner laughed in his hearty fashion. "Some of the old mischief left there yet," said he, catching Flyaway and tossing her to the ceiling. "Have you come here this summer to keep the whole house in commotion? Remember the Charlie boy—don't you—that had the meal-bags tied to his feet?"

"Did he? What for?"

Flyaway had not the least recollection of Charlie; but Horace had talked to her about him, and she said, after a moment's thought,—

"Yes, he washed the pig. Me and Charlie, we played all everything what we thinked about."

"So you did, surely," said a woman who had just come in at the back door, and begun to drop kisses, as sad as tears, on Flyaway's forehead. "Do you know who this is?" Flyaway looked up with a sweet smile, but her mind had lost all impression of her melancholy friend, Miss Whiting. "Look again," said the sad-eyed stranger, who did not like to have even a little child forget her; "you used to call me the 'Polly woman.'"

Katie looked again, and this time very closely.

"There's a great deal o' yellowness in your face," exclaimed she, after a careful survey; "but you was made so!"

Miss Polly laughed drearily. "So you don't remember how I took you out of the watering-trough, you sweet lamb! 'I's tryin' to swim,' you said; 'and that's what is it.' Here's a summer-sweeting for you, dear; do you like them?"

"Yes'm, thank you," said Flyaway, "but I like summer-sourings the best."

At the same time she allowed herself to be taken in Miss Polly's lap, and won that tender-hearted woman's love by putting her arms round her neck, and saying, "Let me kiss you so you'll feel all better. What makes you have tears in your eyes?—tell me."

"We're good friends—I knew we should be," said Miss Polly, quite cheerily. "Look out of the window, and see that swing. How many times I've pushed you and Dotty in that swing when it seemed as if it would break my back!"

Flyaway looked out. There stood the two trees, and between them hung the old swing; but the charm was forgotten. In the field beyond, her eye fell on an object more interesting to her.

"O, O," said she, "I don't see how God could make a man so homebly as that!"

"So homely as what?"

"Why," laughed Dotty, "she means that scarecrow."

The corn was up long ago, but one direful image had still been left to flaunt in the sunlight and soak in the rain.

"That isn't a man," said Prudy; "it's only a great monstrous rag baby, with a coat on."

"Put there to frighten away the crows," added Miss Polly. "When Abner dropped corn in the ground, the great black crows wanted to come and pick it out, and eat it up."

Flyaway frowned in token of strong dislike to the crows. "I wouldn't eat gampa's corn for anything in this world," said she,—"'thout it's popped! 'Cause I don't like it."

Miss Polly laughed quite merrily.

"There," said she, "I've dropped a stitch in my side; it never agrees with me to laugh. I must be going right home, too; but there is one thing more I want to ask you, Katie; do you remember how you ran away, one day, and frightened the whole house, trying to climb up to heaven?"

Katie's face was blank; she had forgotten the journey.

"You passed Jennie Vance and me in the Pines," said Dotty, "and went deep into the woods, and a bee stung you."

"O, now I 'member," said Katie, suddenly. "I 'member the bee as plain as 'tever 'twas!" And she curled her lip with contempt for that small Flyaway, of long ago—that silly baby who had thought heaven was on a hill.

"I went up on a ladder when I was three years old," said Prudy.

"Did you?" said Flyaway. This was a consolation. "Well, I was three years old, too; I didn't know 'bout angels—didn't know they had to have wings on."

Here Flyaway curled her lip again and smiled.

"You are wiser now," sighed Miss Polly. "You and I won't try to go to heaven till our time comes—will we, dear?"

Katie took Miss Polly's large, thin hand, and measured it beside her own tiny one.

"Miss Polly," said she, with one of her extremely wise looks, "when you go up to God you'll be a very little girl!"

"Ah, indeed!" said Miss Polly, weaving the third pin into her shawl; "how do you make that out?"

"Your body'll all be cut off," replied Katie, making the motion of a pair of scissors with her fingers; "all be cut right straight off; there won't be nuffin' left but just your little spirit!"

"Since you know so much, dear, how large is my spirit?"

Katie put her hand on the left side of the belt of her apron.

"Don't you call that small, right under my hand a-beatin'?" said she. "'Bout's big as a bird, Miss Polly. Little round ball for a head, little mites o' eyes; but you won't care—you can see just as well."

"It does beat all where children get such queer ideas—doesn't it, Ruth?" said Miss Whiting.

"Didn't you know it?" cried Katie, finding she had startled Miss Polly. "Didn't you know you's goin' to be little, and fly in the air just so?" throwing up her arms. "I want to go dreffully, for there's a gold harp o' music up there, and I'll play on it: it'll be mine."

"You don't feel in a hurry to die, I hope," said Miss Polly, anxiously.

Katie's eager face clouded. "No," said she, sorrowfully; "I want to, but I hate to go up to God and leave my pink dress. I can't go into it then, I'll be so little."

"You'll be just big enough to go into the pocket," laughed Dotty.

"Hush!" said Miss Polly, gravely; "you shouldn't joke upon such serious subjects. Good by, children. Your house is full of company, and I didn't come to stay. Here's a bag of thoroughwort I've been picking for your grandmother; you may give it to her with my love, and tell her my side is worse. I shall be in to-morrow."

So saying, Miss Polly went away, seeming to be wafted out of the room on a sigh.

The high-chair was brought down from the attic for Flyaway, who sat in it that evening at the tea-table, and smiled round upon her friends in the most benevolent manner.

"I's growing so big now, mamma," said she, coaxingly, "don't you spect I must have some tea?"

Grandmother pleaded for the youngest, too. "Let me give her some just this once, Maria."

"Well, white tea, then," returned Mrs. Clifford, smiling; "and will Flyaway remember not to ask for it again? Mamma thinks little girls should drink milk."

"Yes'm, I won't never. She gives it to me this night, 'cause I's her little grand-girl. Mayn't Hollis have it too, 'cause he's her little grand-boy?"

"Cunning as ever, you see," whispered the admiring Horace to cousin Susy, who replied, rather indifferently,—

"No cunninger than our Prudy used to be."

Flyaway made quick work of drinking her white tea, and when she came to the last few drops she swung her cup round and round, saying,—

"Didn't you know, Hollis, that's the way gampa does, when he gets most froo, to make it sweet?"

No, Horace had not noticed; it was "Fly, with her little eye," who saw everything, and made remarks about it.

"O, O," cried Grace, dropping her knife and fork, and patting her hands softly under the table, "isn't it so nice to be at Willowbrook again, taking supper together? Doesn't it remind you of pleasant things, Susy, to eat grandma's cream toast?'

"Reminds me," said Susy, after reflecting, "of jumping on the hay."

"'Minds me of—of—" remarked Flyaway; and there she fell into a brown study, with her head swaying from side to side.

"I don't know why it is," said Prudy, "but since you spoke, this cream toast makes me think of the rag-bag. Excuse me for being impolite, grandma, but where is the rag-bag?"

"In the back room, dear, where it always is; and you may wheel it off to-morrow."

It had been Mrs. Parlin's custom, once or twice every summer, to allow the children to take the large, heavy rag-bag to the store, and sell its contents for little articles, which they divided among themselves. Sometimes the price of the rags amounted to half or three quarters of a dollar, and there was a regular carnival of figs, candy, and fire-crackers.

Horace was so much older now, that he did not fancy the idea of being seen in the street, trundling a wheelbarrow; but he went on with his cream toast and made no remark.

CHAPTER VI.

THE RAG-BAG.

Next morning there was a loud call from the three Parlins for the rag-bag, in which Flyaway joined, though she hardly knew the difference between a rag-bag and a paper of pins.

"I wish you to understand, girls," said Horace, flourishing his hat, "that I'm not going to cart round any such trash for you this summer."

"Now, Horace!"

"You know, Gracie, you belong to a Girls' Rights' Society. Do you suppose I want to interfere with your privileges?"

"Why, Horace Clifford, you wouldn't see your own sister trundling a wheelbarrow?"

"O, no; I shan't be there," said Horace, coolly; "I shan't see you. I promised to weed the verbena bed for your aunt Louise. Good by, girls. Success to the rag-bag!"

"Let's catch him!" cried Susy, darting after her ungallant cousin but he ran so fast, and flourished his garden hoe so recklessly, that she gave up the chase.

"Let him go," said Grace, with a fine-lady air: "who cares about rag-bags? We've outgrown that sort of thing, you and I, Susy; let the little girls have our share."

"Yes, to be sure," replied Susy, faintly, though not without a pang, for she still retained a childish fondness for jujube paste, and was not allowed a great abundance of pocket-money. "Yes, to be sure, let the little girls have our share."

"Then may we three youngest have the whole rag-bag?" said Prudy, brightly. "Dotty, you and I will trundle the wheelbarrow, and Fly shall go behind."

"What an idea!" exclaimed Grace. "I've seen little beggar children drawing a dog-cart. Grandma'll never allow such a thing."

"Indeed I will," said grandma, tying on her checked apron. "Dog-carts or wheel-barrows, so they only take care not to be rude. In a city it is different."

"Yes, grandma," said Dotty, twisting her front hair joyfully; "but here in the country they want little girls to have good times—don't they? Why don't everybody move into the country, do you s'pose? Lots of bare spots round here,—nothing on 'em but cows."

"Yes, nuffin' but gampa's cows," chimed in Flyaway, twisting her front hair.

"Louisa," said Mrs. Parlin, "you may help me about this loaf of 'Maine plum cake,' and while you are beating the butter and sugar I will look over the rag-bag. Dotty, please run for my spectacles."

When Dotty returned with the spectacles, Jennie Vance came with her, pouting a little at the cool reception she had met, and thinking Miss Dimple hardly polite because she was too much interested in an old rag-bag to pay proper attention to visitors.

"Grandma, what makes you pick over these rags? We can take them just as they are."

"I always do so, my dear, and for several reasons. One is, that woollen pieces may have crept in by mistake. As we profess to sell cotton rags, it would be dishonest to mix them with woollen."

"Yes'm, I understand," said Jennie, who often spoke when it was quite as well to keep silent; "it's always best to be honest—isn't it, Mrs. Parlin?"

The rags were spread out upon the table, giving Flyaway a fine opportunity to scatter them right and left.

"O, here's a splendid piece of blue ribbon to make my doll a bonnet," said Dotty.

"That's another reason why she picks 'em over," remarked Jennie; "so she won't waste things. Only, Dotty, that has got an awful grease-spot."

"There, children," said Mrs. Parlin, presently, "I have taken out a card of hooks and eyes, a flannel bandage, and a shoe-string. You may have everything else."

Dotty caught her grandmother's arm. "Please, grandma, don't sweep 'em into the bag; let us look some more. I've just found a big Lisle glove; if I can find another, then Abner can go blackberrying; he says his hands are ever so tender."

"And you thought he was in earnest," said Prudy. "While you are looking, I'll go into the nursery and finish that holder."

Flyaway, having climbed upon the table, had rolled herself into some mosquito netting, like a caterpillar in a cocoon. They were all so much interested, that grandma, in the kindness of her heart, did not like to disturb them.

"You are welcome to all the treasures you can find, but as soon as the cake is made I shall want the table; so be quick," said she, looking out from the pantry, where she was beating eggs.

"Yes, indeed, grandma, we'll hurry; and may we have every single thing we like the looks of? now, honest."

"Yes, Dotty."

Then Mrs. Parlin and Miss Louise talked about currants, and citron, and quite forgot such trifles as rag-bags.

"Here's another big glove," said Dotty, "not the same color, but no matter; and here are some saddle-bags, Jennie. I'm going to be a doctor."

"Saddle-bags, Dotty! those are pockets." Jennie took them from Miss Dimple's hands. They were held together by a narrow strip of brown linen, and had once belonged to a pair of pantaloons.

"I'm going to see if there isn't something inside," said Jennie. "Why, yes, here's a raisin, true's you live. And here, in the other one,—O, Dotty!"

But Dotty had run into the nursery to show Prudy a muslin cap.

"A wad of—"

Jennie was determined to see what; so she unrolled it.

"Scrip," cried she, holding up some greenbacks.

"Skipt," echoed Flyaway, who had come out of the cocoon and gone into the form of a mop, her head adorned with cotton fringe.

Yes; a two dollar bill and a one dollar bill, as green as lettuce leaves. This was a great marvel. Columbus was not half so much surprised when he discovered America.

"Mrs. Parlin, do you hear?"

But Mrs. Parlin heard nothing, for the din of the egg-beating drowned both the shrill little voices.

A sudden idea came to Jennie. Whose money was this? Mrs. Parlin's? No; hadn't Mrs. Parlin looked over the rags once, and said the children might have what was left? "'You are welcome to all the treasures you can find;' that was what she said," repeated Jennie to herself. "I'm the one that found this treasure,—not Dotty, not Flyaway. This is honest, and I do not lie when I say it."

Jennie began to tremble, and a hot color flew into her cheeks, and added new lustre to her black eyes. "If I could only make Flyaway forget it," thought she, with a whirling sensation of anger towards the innocent child, who knew no better than to proclaim aloud every piece of news she heard. "I'll make her forget it." Jenny hastily concealed the money in the neck of her dress.

"Where's that skipt? that skipt?" said Flyaway.

"Fly Clifford," said Jennie, severely, "you've climbed on the table! Just think of it! Your grandmother doesn't allow you on her table. What made you get up here."

"'Cause," replied Flyaway, seizing the kitty by the tail, and thrusting her into a cabbage-net, "'cause I fought best."

"But you must get right down, this minute."

"No," said Flyaway, shaking her head-dress of white fringe with great solemnity; "I isn't goin' to get down."

"Ah, but you must."

Flyaway opened and shut her eyes slowly, in token of deep displeasure. "I don't never 'low little girls to scold to me," said she. "You'd better call grandma; 'haps she can make me get down."

But it was not Jennie's purpose to wait for that; she seized the little one roughly by the arms, pulled her from the table, and hurried her into the parlor.

Flyaway was indignant. "Does you—feel happy?" said she, with a reproachful glance at Jennie.

"There, look out of the window, Flyaway, darling, and watch to see if Horace isn't coming in from the garden."

"Can't Hollis come, 'thout me watching him?" returned Flyaway, winking slowly again, for her sweet little soul was stirred with wrath. The memory of the "skipt" had indeed been driven away, and she could only think,—

"Isn't Jennie so easy fretted! I wasn't doin' nuffin'; and then she jumped me right down. Unpolite gell! that's one thing."

And Jennie was thinking, "She never'll remember the money now, or, if she does, I don't believe Mrs. Parlin will pay any attention to what she says." Jennie was still very much excited, and wondered why she trembled so.

"I don't mean to keep it unless it's perfectly proper," thought she; "I guess I know the eighth commandment fast enough. I shan't keep it unless Dotty thinks best. I'll tell her, and see what she says."

Jennie had often pilfered little things from her mother's cupboard, such as cake and raisins; but a piece of money of the most trifling value she had never thought of taking before.

Leaving Flyaway busy with block houses, she ran to the nursery door, and motioned with her finger for Dotty to come out.

"What is it?" said Dotty, when they were both shut into the china closet; "don't you want my sister Prudy to know?"

Jennie replied, in a great flutter, "No, no, no. You musn't tell a single soul, Dotty Dimple, as long as you live, and I'll give you half."

"Half what?"

Jennie produced the money from her bosom, feeling, I am glad to say, very guilty. "Out o' those saddle-bag pockets out there," added she, breathlessly; "true's the world."

"Why, Jennie Vance!"

"One had a raisin in and a button, and nobody but me would have thought of looking. You wouldn't—now would you? My father says I've got such sharp eyes!"

"H'm!" said Dotty, who considered her own eyes as bright as any diamonds; "you took the saddle-bag right out of my hand. How do you know I shouldn't have peeked in?"

Jennie did not reply, but smoothed out the wrinkled notes with many a loving pat.

"What did grandma say?" asked Dotty; "wasn't she pleased?"

"Your grandmother doesn't know anything about it, Dotty Dimple; what business is it to her?"

Jennie's tone was defiant. She assumed a courage she was far from feeling.

Dotty was speechless with surprise, but her eyes grew as round as soap-bubbles.

"The pockets don't belong to her, Dotty, and never did. They never came out of any of her dresses—now did they?"

Dotty's eyes swelled like a couple of bubbles ready to burst.

"Jennie Vance, I didn't know you's a thief."

"You stop talking so, Dotty. She was going to sweep everything into the rag-bag—now wasn't she? And this money would have gone in too, if it hadn't been for my sharp eyes—now wouldn't it?"

"But it isn't yours, Jennie Vance—because it don't belong to you."

"Now, Dotty—"

"You go right off, Jennie Vance, and carry it to my grandma this minute."

The tone of command irritated Jennie. She had not felt at all decided about keeping the money, but opposition gave her courage. Her temper and Dotty's were always meeting and striking fire.

"It isn't your grandma's pockets, Miss Parlin. If it was the last word I was to speak, it isn't your grandmother's pockets!"

"Jane Sidney Vance!"

"You needn't call me by my middle name, and stare so at me, Dotty Dimple. I was going to give you half!"

"What do I want of half, when it isn't yours to give?" said Dotty, gazing regretfully at the money, nevertheless. Three dollars! Why, it was a small fortune! If it only did really belong to Jenny!

"Your grandmother said everything we liked the looks of, Dotty. Don't you like the looks of this?"

"But you know, Jennie—"

"O, you needn't preach to me. You wasn't the one that found it. If I'd truly been a thief, or if I hadn't been a thief, it would have been right for me to keep it, and perfectly proper, and not said a word to you, either; so there."

"Jennie Vance, I'm going right out of this closet, and tell my grandma what you've said."

"Wait, Dotty Dimple; let me get through talking. I meant to buy things for your grandmother with it. O, yes, I did—a silk dress, and cap, and shoes."

Dotty twirled her hair, and looked thoughtful.

"Of course I did. Wouldn't it surprise her, when she wasn't expecting it? And Flyaway, too,—something for her. We wouldn't keep anything for ourselves, only just enough to buy clothes and such things as we really need."

Before Dotty had time to reply there was a loud scream from the parlor.

"Fly is killed—she is killed!" cried Dotty; but Jennie had presence of mind enough to tuck the bills into the neck of her dress.

"Don't you tell anybody a word about it, Dotty. If you tell I'll do something awful to you. Do you hear?"

Dotty heard, but did not answer. The fate of her cousin Flyaway seemed more important to her just then than all the bank-bills in the world.

CHAPTER VII.

THE WICKED GIRL.

Flyaway had only been climbing the outside of the staircase, and would have done very well, if some one had not rung the door-bell, and startled her so that she fell from the very top stair to the floor. It was feared, at first, that several bones were broken and her intellect injured for life; but after crying fifteen minutes, she seemed to feel nearly as well as before.

"If ever a child was made of thistle-down it is Flyaway Clifford," said aunt Louise.

Still it was not thought best for her to fatigue herself that day by selling rags, and the wheelbarrow enterprise was put off until the next morning.

The person who rang the door-bell was Mrs. Vance's girl Susan, who called for Jennie to go home and try on a frock. Jennie did not return, and Dotty had a sense of uneasiness all day. The guilty secret of the three dollars weighed upon her mind. Should she, or should she not, tell her grandmother?

"I don't know but Jennie would do something to my things if I told," thought she; "but then I never promised a word. Here it is four o'clock. Who knows but she's gone and spent that money, and my grandmother never'll know what's 'come of it?"

This possibility was very alarming. "Jennie Vance doesn't seem to have any little whisper inside of her heart, that ticks like a watch; but I have. My conscience pricks; so I know that perhaps it's my duty to go and tell."

Dotty drew herself up virtuously and looked in the glass. There she seemed to see an angelic little girl, whose only wish was to do just right—a little girl as much purer than Jennie Vance, as a lily is purer than a very ugly toadstool.

Well, Miss Dotty, there is some truth in the picture. Jennie is not a good child; but neither are you an angel. There is more wickedness in your proud little heart than you will ever begin to find out. And wait a minute. Who teaches you all you know of right and wrong? Is it your mother? Suppose she had died, as did Jennie's mamma, when you were a toddling baby?

There, that's all; you do not hear a word I say; and if you did, you would not heed, O, self-righteous Dotty Dimple!

Dotty ran up stairs to find her grandmother.

"Grandma," whispered she, though there was no one else in the room; "something dreadful has happened. You've lost three dollars!"

"What, dear?"

"O, you needn't look in your pocket. Jennie found 'em in the rag-bag, and tried to make me take half; but of course I never; and now she's run off with 'em!"

"Found three dollars in the rag-bag? I guess not."

"Yes, grandma; for I saw her just as she was going to find em', in a pair of pockets. I should have seen 'em myself if she hadn't looked first."

"Indeed! Is this really so? But she ought to have come and given them to me."

"That was just what I told her, over and over, grandma, and over again. But she's a dreadful naughty girl, Jennie Vance is. If there's anything bad she can do, she goes right off and does it."

"Hush, my child."

"Yes'm, I won't say any more, only I don't think my mother would like to have me play with little girls that take money out of rag-bags."

Dotty drew herself up again in a very stately way.

"Jennie said she was going to buy you a silk dress and so forth; but she does truly lie so, 'one to another,' that you can't believe her for certain, not half she says."

Grandma looked over her spectacles and through the window, as if trying to see what ought to be done.

You can't believe her for certain.

"You did right to tell me this, my child," said she; "but I wish you to say nothing about it to any one else: will you remember?"

"Yes'm," replied Dotty, trying to read her grandmother's face, and feeling a little alarmed by its solemnity. "What you going to do, grandma? Not put Jennie in the lockup—are you? 'Cause if you do—O, don't you! She said 'twas her sharp eyes, and she didn't mean to steal, and 'twasn't your pockets, and she promised she'd give me half—yes, she truly did, grandma."

"Go, dear, and bring me my bonnet from the band-box in my bed-room closet."

Then Mrs. Parlin folded the sheet she was making, put on her best shawl and bonnet, and kid gloves, and taking her sun umbrella, set out for a walk. There was a look in her face which made her little granddaughter think it would not be proper to ask any questions.

Mrs. Parlin met Jennie Vance coming in at the gate.

"O, dear," thought Dotty, "I don't want to see her. Grandma says I've done right, but Jennie'll call me a tell-tale. I'll go out in the barn and hide."

The guilty secret had lain heavy at Jennie's heart all day. As soon as her dress-maker could spare her, and a troublesome little cousin had left, she asked permission to go to Mrs. Parlin's.

"Dotty thinks I meant to keep it," she thought. "I never did see such a girl. You can't say the least little thing but she takes it sober earnest, and says she'll tell her grandmother."

Jennie stole round by the back door, and timidly asked for Miss Dimple.

"I'm sure I don't know where she is," answered Ruthie, with a pleasant smile; "nor Flyaway either. I have been living in peace for half an hour."

Ruthie made you think of lemon candy; she was sweet and tart too.

While Jennie, with the kind assistance of Prudy, was hunting for Dotty, Mrs. Parlin was in Judge Vance's parlor, talking with Jennie's step-mother. Mrs. Vance was shocked to hear of her daughter's conduct, for she loved her and wished her to do right.

"My poor Jennie," said she; "from her little babyhood until she was six years old, there was no one to take care of her but a hired nurse, who neglected her sadly."

"I know just what sort of training Jennie has had from Serena Pond," said Mrs. Parlin; "it was most unfortunate. But you are so faithful with her, my dear Mrs. Vance, that I do believe she will outgrow all those early influences."

"I keep hoping so," said Mrs. Vance, repressing a sigh; "I take it very kindly of you, Mrs. Parlin, that you should come to me with this affair. I shall not allow Jennie to go to your house very often. You do not like to wound my feelings, but I am sure you cannot wish to have your little granddaughter very intimate with a child who is sly and untruthful."

"My dear lady," said grandma Parlin, taking Mrs. Vance's hand, and pressing it warmly; "since we are talking so freely together, and I know you are too generous to be offended, I will confess to you that if Jennie persists in concealing this money, I would prefer not to have Dotty play with her very much; at least while her mother is not here to have the care of her." It was hard for Mrs. Parlin to say this, and she added presently,—

"Please let Jennie spend the night at our house. She may wish to talk with me; we will give her the opportunity."

Mrs. Vance gladly consented. She had observed that Jennie seemed unhappy, and was very anxious to see Dotty again. She hoped she had gone to return the money of her own free will.

When Mrs. Parlin opened the nursery door at home, she found Jennie building block houses, to Flyaway's great delight, while at the other end of the room sat Dotty Dimple, resolutely sewing patchwork.

"O, grandma," spoke up Flyaway, "Jennie came to see me; she didn't come to see Dotty, 'cause Dotty don't want to talk. There, now, Jennie, make a rat to put in the cupboard. R goes first to rat."

Innocent little Flyaway! She had long ago forgotten her pique against Jennie for being "so easy fretted," and jumping her down from the table.

Wretched little Jennie! The new blue and white frock, just finished by her dress-maker, covered a heart filled with mortification. Dotty Dimple would not talk to her. It seemed as if Dotty had climbed to the top of a high mountain, and was looking down, down upon her.

Dotty did feel very exalted to-day; but there was another reason why she would not talk with Jennie: she might have to confess that grandma knew about the money; and then what a scene there would be! So Dotty set her lips together, and sewed as if she was afraid somebody would freeze to death before she could finish her patchwork quilt.

Mrs. Clifford, who did not understand the cause of Dotty's lofty mood, took pity on Jennie, and tried to amuse her. After a while, Dotty came softly along, and sat down close to her aunt Maria, ready to listen to the story of the "Pappoose," though she had heard it fifty times before.

She did not see Jennie alone for one moment. Grandma Parlin did. "Jennie," said she, taking her into the parlor to show her a new shell, "are you going with our little girls, to-morrow, to sell rags?"

"I don't know, ma'am, I'm sure," replied Jennie, looking hard at the sofa. She longed to make an open confession, and get rid of the troublesome money, but had not the courage to do it without some help from Dotty.

"O, dear," thought she, "I feel just as wicked with that money in my bosom! Seems as if she could hear it crumple. If Dotty would only let me talk to her first!"

But Dotty continued as unapproachable as the Pope of Rome. Eight o'clock came, and the two unhappy little girls went slowly up stairs to bed. Dotty, in her lofty pride, tried to make her little friend feel herself a sinner; while Jennie, ready to hide herself in the potato-bin for shame, was, at the same time, very angry with the self-satisfied Miss Dimple. She was awed by her superior goodness, but did not love her any the better for it. Why should she? Dotty's goodness lacked

"Humility, that low, sweet root,

From which all heavenly virtues shoot."

"Here, Miss Parlin," said Jennie, angrily, as she took off her dress; "here it is, right in my neck. I should have gone and given it to your grandmother, ever so long ago, if you hadn't acted so!"

Dotty pulled off her stockings.

"I 'spose you thought I was going to keep it. Here, take your old money!"

"You did mean to keep it, Jane Sidney Vance," retorted Dotty, as fierce as a thistle; and finished undressing at the top of her speed.

The money lay on the floor, and neither of the proud girls would pick it up. Jennie, who always prayed at her mother's knee, forgot her prayer to-night, and climbed into bed without it. But Dotty, feeling more than ever how much better she was than her little friend, knelt beside a chair, and prayed in a loud voice. First, she repeated the "Lord's Prayer," then "Gentle Jesus, meek and mild," and "Now I lay me down to sleep." She was not talking to her heavenly Father, but to Jennie, and ended her petitions thus:—

"O God, forgive me if I have done anything naughty to-day, and please forgive Jennie Vance, the wickedest girl in this town."

Then the little Pharisee got into bed.

CHAPTER VIII.

"WHEELBARROWING."

"The wickedest girl in this town!" Jennie's eyes flashed in the dark like a couple of fireflies. At first she was too angry to speak; and when words did come, they were too weak. She wanted words that were so strong, and bitter, and fierce, that they would make Dotty quail. But all she could say was,—

"O, dreadful good you are, Miss Parlin! Good's the minister! Ah! guess I'll get out and sleep on the floor!"

Dotty made no reply, but rolled over to the front of the bed, and Jennie pushed herself to the back of it. There the little creatures lay in silence, each on an edge of the bedstead, and a whole mattress between. Sleep did not come at once.

"She's left that money on the floor," thought Dotty; "what if a mouse should creep down the chimney, and gnaw it all up? But she must take care of it herself. I shan't!"

And Jennie thought, wrathfully, "Dotty says such long prayers she can't stop to pick up that scrip! If she expects me to get out of bed, she's made a mistake; I won't touch her old money."

About nine o'clock grandma Parlin came quietly into the room with a lamp. A smile crept round the corners of her mouth, as she saw the little girls sleeping so widely apart, their faces turned away from each other.

"How is this?" said she, as the two bills caught her eye. "Of all the foolish children! Dropping money about the room like waste paper!"

The light awoke Jennie, who had only just fallen asleep. "Now is the time," said she to herself; and without waiting for a second thought, which would have been a worse one, she sprang out of bed, and caught Mrs. Parlin by the skirts.

"That money is yours, Mrs. Parlin," said she, bravely. "Yours; I found it in the rag-bag. Something naughty came into me this morning, and made me want to keep it; but I'm ever so sorry, and never'll do it again. Will you forgive me?"

Then grandma Parlin seated herself in a rocking-chair, took Jennie right into her lap, and talked to her a long while in the sweetest way. Jennie curled her head into the good woman's neck, and sobbed out all her wretchedness.

"She knew she was real bad, and people didn't like to have her play with their little girls, and Dotty Dimple thought she was awful; but was she the wickedest girl in this town?"

"No; O, no!"

"Wasn't Dotty some bad, too?"

"Yes, Dotty often did wrong."

Then Jenny wept afresh.

"She knew she was worse than Dotty, though. She wished,—O, dear, as true as she lived,—she wished she was dead and buried, and drowned in the Red Sea, and the grass over her grave, and shut up in jail, and everything else."

Then Mrs. Parlin soothed her with kind words, but told the truth with every one.

"No 'm," Jennie said; "it wasn't right to take fruit-cake without leave, or tell wrong stories either; she wouldn't any more. Yes'm, she would try to be good—she never had tried much.—Yes 'm, she would ask God to help her. Should you suppose He would do it?

"Yes 'm, she would ask Him not to let her have much temptation. She did believe she would rather be a good girl—a real good girl, like Prudy, not like Dotty!—than to have a velvet dress with spangles all over it."

All this while Dotty did not waken. In the morning she was surprised to see her little bedfellow looking so cheerful.

"I've told your grandmother all about it," said Jennie with a smile. 'I knew I did wrong, but I don't believe I should have meant to if you hadn't acted so your own self—now that's a fact."

"You haven't seen my grandmother," returned Dotty, not noticing the last clause of her friend's remark. "You dreamed it."

"No, she came in here and forgave me. She's the best woman in this world. What do you think she said about you, Dotty Dimple? She said there were other little girls full as good as you are. There!"

"O!"

"Said you 'often did wrong,' that's just what," added Jennie, correcting herself, and making sure of the "white truth."

Step by step Dotty came down from the mountain-top, and, before breakfast was ready, had led her visitor through the morning dew to the playhouse under the trees, chatting all the way as if nothing had happened.

It proved that the money belonged to Abner. He had missed it several weeks before, and ever since that had been suspecting old Daniel McQuilken, a day laborer, of stealing it.

"I'm ashamed of it now," said Abner to Ruth, "though I didn't tell anybody but you. I wish you'd mix a pitcher of sweetened water, and let me take it out to the field to old Daniel. I feel as if I wanted to make it up to him some way."

Ruth laughed; and when Abner came into the house at ten o'clock, she had a pitcher of molasses and water ready for him, also a plate of cherry turnovers. Flyaway insisted upon toddling over the ground with one of the turnovers in her apron.

"Man," said she, when they reached the field, and she saw the Irishman with his funny red and white hair, "what's your name, man?"

He wiped his face with his checked shirt-sleeve, and took a turnover from her hand, bowing very low as he did so.

"Thank ee, my little lady; sense you're plazed to ask me,—my name's Dannul."

"O, are you?" said Flyaway, looking up in surprise at the large and oddly-dressed stranger. "Are you Daniel? My mamma's just been reading about you. You was in the lions' den—wasn't you, Daniel?"

Mr. McQuilken smiled at bareheaded, flossy-haired little Katie, and replied, with a wink at Abner,—

"Fath, little lady, and I suppose I'm that same Dannul; but 'twas so long ago I've clane forgot aboot it entirely."

"O, did you? Well, you was in the lions' den, Daniel, but they didn't bite you, you know, 'cause you prayed so long and so loud, with your winners up; and then God wouldn't let 'em bite."

Old Daniel laid both his huge hands on Katie's head.

"Swate little chirrub," said he, "don't she look saintish?"

Katie moved away; she did not like to have her hair pulled, and Daniel was unconsciously drawing it through the big cracks in his fingers, as if he was waxing silk.

"I guess I'll go home now," said she, with a timid glance at the man whom the lions did not bite; "they'll be spectin' me."

Abner and Daniel both watched the tiny figure across the fields till Ruth came out to meet it, and it fluttered into the east door of the house.

"There, she's safe," said Abner; "she needs as much looking after as a young turkey."

"She runs like a little sperrit, bliss her swate eyes," said Daniel. "I had one as pooty as her, but she's at Mary's fate, Hivven rist her sowl!"

The moment Flyaway reached the house, she rushed into the parlor to tell her mother the news.

"The man you readed about in the book, mamma, he's out there! Daniel, that the lions didn't bite, mamma, 'cause he prayed so long and so loud with his winners up; he's out there—got a hat on."

"O, no, my child; it is thousands of years since Daniel was in the lions' den; he died long and long ago."

"But he said he did, mamma; he told me so. I fought he was dead mamma, but he said he wasn't."

Mrs. Clifford shook her head. "I dare say his name is Daniel, but he was never in a lion's den."

Flyaway opened and closed her eyes in the slowest and most impressive manner. "Mamma," said she, solemnly, "does—folks—tell—lies?"

It was an entirely now idea to the innocent child: it stamped itself upon her mind like a motto on warm sealing-wax, "Folks—does—tell—lies."

Mrs. Clifford was sorry to see the look of distrust on the young face

"Listen to me, little Flyaway. I think the man was in sport; he was only playing with you, as Horace does sometimes, when he calls himself your horse."

Flyaway said no more, but she pressed her eyelids together again, and felt that she had been trifled with. Half an hour afterwards Prudy heard her repeating, slowly, to herself, "Folks—does—tell—lies."

"Why, here she is," called Dotty from the piazza; "come, Fly; we're going wheel-barrowing."

"Wait a minute, cousin Dotty," said Mrs. Clifford; "Flyaway must put on a clean frock; she is not coming home with you, but you are to leave her at aunt Martha's. I shall meet her there at dinner time."

"O, mamma, may I? I love you a hundred rooms full. Let me go bring my buttoner bootner quick's a minute."

Flyaway was not long in getting ready. She was never long about anything.

"You said we might have all the money, we three—didn't you, grandma?" asked Dotty again, at the last moment, thinking how glad she was Jennie had gone home, and would not claim a share.

"Yes," replied patient grandma for the fifth time; "you may do anything you like with it, except to buy colored candy."

As they were trundling the wheelbarrow out of the yard, Horace came up from the garden.

"Prudy," said he, with rather a shame-faced glance at his favorite cousin, "you girls will cut a pretty figure, parading through the streets like a gang of pedlers. Come, let me be the driver."

"O, we thought you couldn't leave your flower-beds, sir," replied Prudy, sweeping a courtesy.

"Well, the weeds are pretty tough, ma'am; roots 'way down in China, and the Emperor objects to parting with 'em; but—"

"Poh! we don't need any boys," cried the self-sustained Miss Dimple; "if your hands are too soft, Prudy, you mustn't push. Wait and see what Dotty Dimple can do."

"O, then, if you spurn me and my offer, good by. I suppose my little Topknot goes for surplusage," said Horace, who liked now and then to puzzle Dotty with a new word. He meant that Flyaway was of no use, but rather in the way.

"No, she needn't do any such thing," returned Dotty. "Jump in, Fly, and sit on the bag." And off moved the gay little party, "the middle-aged sister" laughing so she could hardly push, Flyaway dancing up and down on the rag-bag, like a humming-bird balancing itself on a twig; Grace and Susy looking down from the "green chamber" window, and saying to each other, with wounded family pride, "Should you think grandma would allow it?" Out in the street the young rag-merchants were greeted by a cow lowing dismally. Flyaway, in her rustic carriage, felt as secure as the fabled "kid on the roof of a house;" so she called out, "Don't cry, old cow; I 'shamed o' you."

At this Prudy and Dotty laughed harder than ever.

"'Sh right up, old cow," said Flyaway, standing on her "tipsy-toes," and making a threatening gesture with her little arms; "'Sh right up!—O, why don't that cow mind in a minute?"

In her earnestness the little girl pushed the bag to one side, and Prudy and Dotty, shaking with laughter, tipped over the wheelbarrow. No harm was done except to give Flyaway a dust-bath in her nice clean frock. Just as they were struggling with the bag, to get it in again, they were overtaken by a droll-looking equipage. It was a long house on wheels, and instantly reminded Dotty of Noah's ark.

"O, a house a-ridin'! a house a-ridin'!" exclaimed Flyaway, gazing after it with the greatest astonishment.

Dotty thought the world was going topsy-turvy. She looked at the trees to see if they stood fast in the ground. But Prudy explained it as soon as she could stop laughing.

"Only a photograph saloon," said she. "Didn't you ever see one before? We don't have them in the city going round so, but things are different in the country. Let's watch and see where it stops."

"O, dear me," said Dotty; "I shouldn't want to live in a house that couldn't stand still! Stove tipping over, and the gingerbread falling out of the oven! There, I declare!"

The look of wonder on Dotty's face was so amusing that Prudy was obliged to hold on to her sides.

"There, look!" said she; "it has stopped down by the corner. Now the man can bake his gingerbread if he wants to, and the stove won't tip over. Jump in, Flyaway, and finish your ride."

"No-o," said Flyaway, wavering between her fear of the cow, some yards ahead, and her fear of the rocking, unsteady wheelbarrow. "Guess I won't get in no more, Prudy; it wearies me."

"Wearies you?"

"Yes: don't you know what 'wearies' means, Prudy? It means it makes me a—a—little—scared!"

And in her "weariness" Flyaway nestled between her two cousins, and kept fast hold of their skirts till the cow was safely passed and the red store reached.

"Bravo!" exclaimed Mr. Bradley, the merchant, as he came out and dragged the rag-bag into the store; "so you've taken the business into your own hands, my little women? Ah, this is a progressive age! Walk in—walk in."

Prudy blushed, Dotty smiled, and Flyaway took off her hat, as she usually did when she did not know what else to do.

"Take some seats, young ladies," said Mr. Bradley, placing three chairs in a row, and bowing as if to the most distinguished visitors. Two or three men, who were lounging about the counter, looked on with a smile. Dotty was very well satisfied, for she enjoyed attention; but Prudy, who was older, and had a more delicate sense of propriety, blushed and cast down her eyes. She had thought nothing of driving a wheelbarrow through the street, but now, for the first time, a feeling of mortification came over her. If Mr. Bradley would only keep quiet!

"A fine morning, my young friends! Rather warm, to be sure. And so you have brought rags to sell? Would you like the money for them, or do you think we can make a trade with some articles out of the store?"

"Grandma said we could have the money between us, we three," replied Dotty, with refreshing frankness, "and buy anything we please except red and yellow candy."

"I want a music," said Flyaway, in an eager whisper; "a music, and a ollinge, and a pig."

"Hush!" said Prudy, for the man with a piece of court-plaster on his cheek was certainly laughing.

Mr. Bradley took the bag into another room to weigh it. A boy was in there, drawing molasses. "James," said Mr. Bradley, "run down cellar, and bring up some beer for these young ladies."

There was a smile on James's face as he drove the plug into the barrel. Prudy saw it through the open door, and it went to her heart. The cream beer was excellent, but Prudy did not relish it. She and Dotty had been whispering together.

"We will take two thirds of the rags in money, if you please," said Prudy, in such a low tone that Mr. Bradley had to bend his ear to hear.

"Because," added Dotty, who wished to have everything clearly explained, "because we want to have our tin-types taken, sir. We saw a saloon riding on wheels, and we thought we'd go there, and see if the man wasn't ready to take pictures."

"And our little cousin may use her third, and buy something out of the store, if you please," said the blushing Prudy.

CHAPTER IX.

TIN-TYPES.

Mr. Bradley said he did not often allow any one behind his counter, as all the boys in the village could testify; but these young ladies were welcome in any part of the store.

"That little one is the spryest child I ever saw," said the man with the court-plaster, as Flyaway hovered about the candy-jars, like a butterfly over a flower-bed. "She isn't a Yankee child—is she?"

"No, sir," replied Dotty, quickly; "she is a westerness."

She had heard Horace use the word, and presumed it was correct.

"I do wish Dotty would be more afraid of strangers," thought Prudy. "I never will take her anywhere again—with a wheelbarrow."

Flyaway fluttered around for a minute, and then alighted upon her favorite sweet-meats, "pepnits." She chose for her portion a large amount of these, an harmonica, and a sugar pig, which Dotty assured her was not 'colored." "Nothing but pink dots, and those you can pick off."

"The rags came to seventy-five cents, and this young lady has now had her third; here is the remainder," said Mr. Bradley, smiling as he gave each of the little Parlins some money, and bowed them out of the store.

"I'll put it in my porte-monnaie, sir; my sister Prudy didn't bring hers.'

"What makes you talk so much, Dotty Dimple?" said Prudy, "that man has been making sport of us all the time."

"Did he?" said Dotty, solemnly. "I'm 'stonished at grandma Parlin letting us sell rags! Wish this wheelbarrow was in the Stiftic Ocean."

"But it isn't, little sister, and the worst of it is, we've got to take it to the photograph saloon; it's so far home and back again."

"Got to take the ole wheelbarrel every single where we go," pouted Flyaway, as drearily as either of her cousins.

"You needn't mind it, though," said Dotty, giving the one-wheeled coach a hard push; "a little girl that's going visiting, and have succotash for dinner."

"I didn't know I was. O, I am so glad! What is it!"

"Corn and beans. Aunt Martha's girl is the best cook,—makes cherry pudding. Dear, dear, dear! Wish I was in Portland; see 'f I wouldn't go to Tate Penny's, and have some salmon and ice-cream!"

Down the beautiful shaded street walked the three little rag-pedlers; and it did seem as if they were met by all the people in town, from the minister down to the barefoot boys going fishing. At last they arrived at the house on wheels.

"Now I'll tell you, Fly, what we're going to do," said Prudy. "Dotty and I want to have our tin-types taken, to give to grandma, as a pleasant surprise. We'll pay for yours too, if you'll sit for it."

"Tin-tybe? Of course, indeed I will. Won't I have nuffin to do but just sit still? But I'd rather be gentle (generous), and give it to my mamma."

"Well, to your mamma, then. What will be the harm, Dotty, in leaving this wheelbarrow out here at the door?"

"I don't know," said Dotty; "I hope there won't any 'bugglers' come along, and steal it."

"I shall watch it," replied Prudy, with a care-worn look; and they all went up the steps and entered the little picture-gallery.

The windows were closed, and the odor of chemicals was so stifling, that the children almost gasped for breath. The artist seemed glad to see them, made no remarks about the wheelbarrow, though he must have noticed it, and said he would be ready in a few minutes. While they waited, they walked about the room, looking at the pictures on the walls.

"See," said Dotty; "there is Abby Grant, with her hair frizzed. Prudy" (in a low whisper), "you don't s'pose he will carry us off—do you? I forgot about the wheels, or I wouldn't have come! O, see that little boy; hands as big as my father's! Here comes Jennie Vance; I'm going to call her in."

Dotty had forgotten her contempt for her lively friend. Jennie came in, twirling the rim of her hat, and looking quite gratified by this mark of friendship in Dotty.

"Going to have your picture taken, Dotty Dimple? Well, so I would if I was as pretty as you are. O, dear" (with a sly peep at the glass), "I wish I wasn't so homely."

Now Jennie was a handsome child, and knew it well; but Dotty took her wail in earnest. "Why, Jennie," said she, with ready sympathy, "I don't think you're so very homely; not half so homely, any way, as some of the girls at Portland."

Jennie frowned and bit her thumb. Prudy smiled "behind her mouth," but Dotty was serenely unconscious that she had given offence. By this time the artist was ready, and thought it best to try Flyaway first; for he had had enough experience with children to see at a glance that this one would be as difficult to "take" as a bird on the wing. Prudy made sure the wheelbarrow was safe, and then turned to arrange her little cousin.

"Here, put your hands down in your lap."

Up went the little hands to the flossy hair. "It won't stay, Prudy, or nelse you tie it."

"I shall brush it, the very last minute, Flyaway. All you must do is sit still. Mayn't she look at your watch, sir, just to keep her eyes from moving?"

"No matter what she looks at," replied the artist; "but she must keep that little head of hers straight."

His tone was firm; he hoped to awe her into quietness. Flyaway was frightened, and clung to Prudy for protection. "Don't the gempum love little gee—urls?" said she, in a voice as low and sad as a dying dove's.

Mr. Poindexter laughed, and stroked the beautiful floss lovingly.

"Just turn your sweet little face this way, dear child; that's all."

"O, my shole! Must I turn my face to my back!" said Flyaway, bewildered.

"No, no; look at this picture on the wall. See what it is, so you can tell your mother."

"It's a bridge, and a man, and a fish," said Flyaway, flashing a glance at it.

"There, smooth your forehead; now you will do." And so she did for two seconds, till she began to squint, to see whether it was a fish or a dog; and that picture was spoiled.

Next time she tried so very hard to sit still that she swayed to and fro like a slender-stemmed flower when the wind goes over it. The picture was blurred.

"O, Fly, you must keep your shoulders still," said Prudy, looking as anxious as the old woman in the shoe.

"I didn't never want to come here," said the child; "when I sit so still, Prudy, it 'most gives me a pain."

"But you haven't sat still yet, not a minute."

"I could, you know, Prudy, or nelse I didn't have to breeve," groaned Flyaway, lifting her eyebrows.

"Another one spoiled," said the artist, trying to smile.

"Yes," said Dotty, who felt none of the care. "Once it was her head, and then it was her shoulders; and now her eyebrows are all of a quirk."

Poor little Flyaway felt as much out of place as a grape-vine would feel, if it had to make believe it was a pine tree.

"Wisht I'd said 'no,' 'stead o' 'yes,'" murmured she, puckering her mouth to the size of a very small button-hole.

"This will never do," said the patient artist, almost in despair. "Hold your little chin up, there's a lady. Don't put it in your neck. Now! Ready!"

But at the critical moment there was a jerk, and Flyaway cried out,—

"I've got a sneeze; but, O, dear, I can't sneeze it."

"Why, where's that head of yours, little Tot? I declare, I believe it goes on wires, like a jumping-jack."

"My head's wrong side up," said Flyaway, mournfully; "my mother said it was."

Mr. Poindexter laughed: it was impossible to be vexed with such a gentle child as Flyaway. "Really, my young friends," said he, rubbing his stained fingers through his hair, "I believe I shall be obliged to give it up for the present. Have the child's mother come with her to-morrow, and we'll do better, I am sure."

With the likenesses of the other girls he succeeded very well; and Prudy and Dotty were glad to find, that after paying for theirs, they each had ten cents left.

"Now, Fly, we will go to aunt Martha's."

But Fly was amusing herself by scraping dirt out of the cracks of her boots with a bit of glass.

"Dotty won't be to aunt Marfie's. I don't want to stay where Dotty isn't."

"But your mamma will be there, you know; and I told you what they are going to have for dinner."

"Yes, secretary," said Flyaway, proud of her memory. "She is a very nice cooker, but you'll have hard work to get me to go."

She drawled out the words languidly, and seemed on the point of going to sleep.

"O, girls, girls, girls," cried Prudy, opening the door and looking out, "our wheelbarrow is gone—it's gone!"

"It's bugglers; I told you so," said Dotty.

Mr. Poindexter was quite amused by his little sitters. "I saw that you came in a coach," said he, "and without any horses."

"Our grandmother said we might," spoke up Dotty, anxious to divert all blame from herself. "She said we might; but Prudy ought to have gone straight home. I knew it all the time."

"I dare say some one has driven off your carriage in sport," said the kind-hearted photographer; "never fear."

"O, no, sir; it was new and red. Folks wanted it to haul stones in, and that was why they took it," said Dotty, wrathfully.

The children looked up street and down street. No wheelbarrow in sight. "We must go to aunt Martha's, and then come back and hunt for it, if we have to go without our dinners," they said. They took Flyaway between them, and marched her off. She was almost as passive as a rag baby, ready to drop down anywhere, and fall asleep. "'Cause I am so tired," said she.

Aunt Martha cordially invited the two cousins to dine. They thanked her, but no, they must find the wheelbarrow. "We shan't say, certain positive, that bugglers took it, but we s'pose so," said Dotty, softening her judgment, as she remembered her mistake about the "screw-up pencil." They went home through the broiling sun, but found no trace of the wheelbarrow.

"It's a dreadful thing," said Prudy, lazily, "but I don't feel as bad as I should if I was fairly awake."

"Me, too," yawned Dotty; "I wish we could lie down under the trees, and go to sleep."

They had been a long while in the close saloon, inhaling ether, and this was the cause of their languor. As they entered the yard they met Horace.

"O, dear," said Dotty, trying to look as sorry as she knew she ought to feel, "that wheel—"

"What!" exclaimed Prudy.

There, under a syringa tree in the garden, stood the wheelbarrow. The girls rubbed their eyes, and wondered if they were walking in their sleep.

"That thing trundled itself in here about half an hour ago," said Horace, gravely. "You may know I was surprised to look up, and see it coming without hands, just rolling along like a velocipede."

Dotty eyed the runaway wheelbarrow stupidly. "I don't believe it," said she, flatly.

Horace laughed; and then the fog cleared away from Dotty's mind in a minute.

"Why, girls," said he, "how long did you think I could wait to haul off my weeds? You were gone two hours. I watched you on your parade, and followed at a respectful distance."

"There, Horace Clifford!"

"In order not to disturb the procession. Then, when I saw you going into the saloon, I went up and claimed my wheelbarrow. Didn't want it any longer—did you?"

"No, and never want it again," said Prudy.

"By the way, here's a conundrum for you, girls, Why's a wheelbarrow like a potato?"

"I shouldn't think it was like it at all," answered Dotty. "Where did you read that?"

"Didn't read it anywhere. I've given up books since I undertook gardening. Never was much of a bookworm. Make a very respectable earth-worm; ask aunt Louise if I don't."

The little girls entered the house, too tired and sleepy to make any reply.

CHAPTER X.

WAKING.

Flyaway was very much sleepier than either of her cousins, and really did not know where she was, or what she was doing. Lonnie Adams, a boy of Horace's age, tried to interest her. He made believe the old cat was a sheep, killed her with an iron spoon, and hung her up by the hind legs for mutton, all which Pussy bore like a lamb, for she had been killed a great many times, and was used to it. But it did not please Flyaway; neither did aunt Martha's collection of shells and pictures call forth a single smile. There was a beautiful clock in the parlor, and the pendulum was in the form of a little boy swinging; but Flyaway would not have cared if it had been a gallows, and the boy hanging there dead.

Uncle John took her on his knee, asked her what her name was, where she lived, and whom she loved best; but she only answered she "didn't know." She might have been Daniel in the lions' den, or Joseph in the pit, for all the difference to her.

"How very singular!" said aunt Martha. "I wish her mother would come. Do feel her pulse, John, and see if it is fever."

"Nothing of the kind," said uncle John, as the little one's head dropped on his shoulder. "Overcome by the heat; that's all. I'll just lay her down on the sofa."

When Mrs. Clifford came, she was surprised to find the child fast asleep. She would not have her wakened for dinner; so Flyaway missed her "secretary." But when it was three o'clock, and she still slept, Mrs. Clifford feared something was wrong, and decided to take her home. Uncle John had "Lightning Dodger" harnessed, and brought around to the door.

"Wake up, little daughter," said Mrs. Clifford; "we are going home now."

Flyaway looked around vacantly, her eyes as heavy as drenched violets.

"You must come again, and stay longer," said aunt Martha; "it is hardly polite not to let little girls have their dinners—do you think it is?'

"Yes 'm," replied Flyaway, faintly. She did not understand a word any one said; it all sounded as indistinct as the roaring of a sea-shell. By the time she was lifted into her mother's arms in the carriage, she was nodding again. When they reached home she scarcely spoke, but, dropping upon the sofa, went on with her dreams. It was odd for Flyaway to take a nap in the daytime, and such a long one as this!

"It must be a very warm day," said Mrs. Parlin, "for Prudy and Dotty have been asleep too."

"Where did they go after they sold the rags?" asked Mrs. Clifford; "they all look pale."

"To a photograph saloon. Here are the tin-types they brought home to me," replied grandma, producing them from her pocket, with a gratified smile.

"Very good, mother—don't you think so? I would be glad to have as truthful a likeness of our little Katie; but she must be taken asleep. I wonder, by the way, if there wasn't something in the air of the saloon which made the children all so languid?"

"Why, yes, Maria; very likely it was the ether. Now you speak of it, I am confident it must have been the ether."

"I knew just such an instance before," said Mrs. Clifford; "and that is why I happened to think of it now."

About four o'clock Flyaway came to her senses.

"Where's the wheelbarrel?" said she, rubbing her eyes.

"O, Horace came and took it," said Dotty. "Hasn't this been the queerest day!"

"You said you's goin' to take me to aunt Marfie's; why didn't you?"

"O, we did; we took you, you know."

"Dotty Dimpul, I shouldn't think you'd make any believe."

"I'm not 'making any believe'—am I, Prudy?"

"No, Fly, she isn't. We pulled you along,—don't you remember?—and you hung back, and said, 'I am so tired.'"

"I don't 'member," said Flyaway, slowly and sadly. "I shouldn't think you'd make any believe, Prudy."

"We'll ask your mamma, then; she tells the truth. Aunt 'Riah, didn't we take Flyaway to aunt Martha's this morning, and didn't you go there too?"

"Certainly," said Mrs. Clifford; "but it wasn't much of a visit,—was it, darling!—when you slept most of the time, and didn't have a mouthful of dinner?"

Flyaway sighed heavily, and looked at her mother. "O, mamma! mamma!"

"What is it, dear?"

"O, mamma," repeated she, sorrowfully, "why did you say those words?"

"What words, darling?"

"Those naughty, naughty words, mamma." Flyaway's gentle eyes were afloat. She crossed the room, and knelt by Mrs. Clifford's chair, looking up at her with an expression of anguish.

"That man, he wasn't in the lions' den, that prayed so long and so loud, mamma."

"Well, dear."

"He telled a wrong story to me, mamma."

"My darling baby," said Mrs. Clifford, catching Flyaway in her arms, "do you think your own dear mother is telling you a wrong story this minute?"

"'Cause, 'cause, mamma, I didn't go to aunt Marfie's!"

"Yes, you did, my precious daughter; but you were asleep and dreaming. We brought you home in the carriage, and you didn't know it. Can't you believe it because I say so?"

Flyaway made no reply except to curl her head under Mrs. Clifford's arm, like a frightened chicken under its mother's wing. Mrs. Clifford looked troubled. She was afraid the little one could not be made to understand it. Horace came to her aid.

"Hold up your head, little Topknot, and hear brother talk. Once there were three little girls, and they all travelled round with a wheelbarrow. By and by they came to a man's house on wheels."

"Yes," said Flyaway, starting up; "I 'member."

"And the wee girl, with dove's eyes—"

"O, O, that's me!"

"She couldn't keep still, and couldn't get any picture."

"No, tin-tybe; 'cause—'cause—"

"And all the while there was something in the man's house they kept breathing into their noses, and it made them grow sleepy."

"Just so?" asked Flyaway, sniffing.

"Yes; and by and by the little one with dove's eyes was as stupid as that woman you saw lying down in the street with the pig looking at her."

"Me? Was I a drunken?" said Flyaway, in a subdued tone.

"O, no," put in Dotty; "it wasn't whiskey, it was either; and I didn't know much more than you did, Fly Clifford. That was why I lost your money, Prudy; I just about know it was."

Flyaway began to understand. The look of fear and distrust went out of her eyes, and she threw her arms round her mother's neck, kissing her again and again.

"'Haps I did go to aunt Marfie's, mamma; 'haps I was asleep!"

"That's right, Miss Topknot," cried Horace; "now your brother'll carry you pickaback."

A little while afterward Mrs. Clifford began a letter to her husband.

"I am going to tell papa about his little girl—that she is very well."

"O, no, you needn't, mamma," said Flyaway, laughing; "papa knows it. I was well at home."

"What shall I tell him, then?"

Flyaway thought a moment.

"Tell him all the folks doesn't tell lies," said she, earnestly; "only but the naughty folks tells lies."

So that was settled; and Flyaway decided to write off the whole story, and send to her father—a mixture of little sharp zigzags, curves, and dots. When Horace asked her what these meant, she said "she couldn't 'member now; but papa would know."

There was another matter which troubled grandma Parlin somewhat. Dotty had gone to the store, after dinner, with two ten-cent pieces in her porte-monnaie. She had bought for herself some jujube paste, but in returning had lost the other dime.

"Grandma, do you think that is fair?" said Prudy. "She has lost my money, but she doesn't care at all; only laughs. I was going to put it with some more I had, and buy mother a collar."

"No, it is not right," replied grandma. "I will talk with her, and try to make her willing to give you some of hers in return."

Ah, grandma Parlin, you little knew what you were undertaking when you called Dotty Dimple into the back parlor next morning, and began to talk about that money! Children's minds are strange things. They are like bottles with very small necks; and when you pour in an idea, you must pour very slowly, a drop at a time, or it all runs over. Dotty did not know much more about money than Flyaway.

"My child," said her grandmother, "it seems you have lost something which belonged to Prudy."

Dotty looked up carelessly from the picture of a rose she held in her hand, which she meant to adorn with yellow paint.

"O, yes 'm; you mean that money."

"There are several things you don't know, Dotty; and one is, that you have no right to lose other people's things."

"No 'm."

"The money you dropped out of your porte-monnaie, yesterday, was Prudy's, not yours; and what are you going to do about it?"

"Let me see; my mother'll come to-morrow; I'll ask her to give me some more."

"But is that right? Dotty lost the money; must not Dotty be the one to give it back?"

"O, grandma, I can't find it! The wind blew it away, or a horse stepped on it. I can't find it, certainly."

"No; but you have money of your own. You can give some of that to Prudy."

"Why-ee!" moaned Dotty. "Prudy's got ever so much. O, grandma, she has; and my box is so empty it can't but just jingle."

"But, my dear, that has nothing to do with the case. If Prudy has a great deal of money, you have no right to lose any of it. Don't you think you ought to give it back?"

"O, no, grandma—I don't; because she doesn't need it! I wish she'd give me ten cents, for I do need it; I haven't but a tinty, tonty mite."

Here Dotty threw herself on the sofa, the picture of despair. Grandma was perplexed. Had she been pouring ideas into Dotty's mind too fast? What should she say next?

"My dear little girl, suppose Prudy should lose some of your money—what then?"

"I shouldn't like it at all, grandma. Don't let her go to my box—will you?"

"Selfish little girl!" said grandma, looking keenly at Dotty's troubled face. "You would expect Prudy to return every cent, if she were in your place."

"Because—because—grandma—"

"Yes; and when I explain your duty to you, you don't understand me. You would understand if you were not so selfish!"

Dotty winced.

"Don't come to me again, and complain of Jennie Vance."

Dotty could not meet her grandmother's searching gaze: it seemed to cut into her heart like a sharp blade.

"Am I as bad as Jennie Vance? Yes, just us bad; and grandma knows it. But then," said she aloud, though very faintly, "Prudy needn't have put it in my porte-monnaie; she might have known I'd lose it."

"Dotty, I am not going to say any more about it now. You may think it over to-day, and decide for yourself whether you are following the Golden Rule. Or, if you choose, you may wait and talk with your mother."

"Yes 'm." Dotty was glad to escape into the kitchen.

CHAPTER XI.

AUNT POLLY'S STORY.

Flyaway sat on the kitchen floor, feeding Dinah with a roasted apple. As often as Dinah refused a teaspoonful, she put it into her own mouth, saying, with a wise nod, "My child, she's sick; hasn't any appletite."

Out of doors it was raining heartily. It seemed as if the "upper deep" was tipping over, and pouring itself into the lap of the earth.

"O, Ruthie," sighed Dotty Dimple, "my mother won't come while it's such weather. Do you s'pose 'twill ever clear off?" [Blank Page]

Flyaway and Dinah.

Flyaway and Dinah.

"Yes, I do," replied Ruth, trimming a pie briskly; "it only began last night at five."

"Why, Ruthie Dillon! it began three weeks ago, by the clock! Don't you know that day I couldn't go visiting? Only sometimes it stops a while, and then begins again."

"If you're going to have the blues, Miss Dotty, I'll thank you kindly just to take yourself out of this kitchen. Polly Whiting is here, and she is as much as a body can endures in this dull weather."

"It's pitiful 'bout the rain, Dotty; but you mustn't scold when God sended it," said Flyaway, dropping the feeble Dinah, and pursuing her cousin round the room with a pin. In a minute they were both laughing gayly, till Flyaway caught herself on her little rocking-chair, and "got a torn in her apron." That ended the sport.

"What shall I do to make myself happy?" said Dotty, musingly; for she wished to put off all thought of Prudy's money. "I should like to roll out some thimble-cookies, but Ruthie hasn't much patience this morning. I never dare do things when her lips are squeezed together so."

But Flyaway dared do things. She took up the kitty, and played to her on the "music," till Ruth's ears were "on edge." After this the harmonica fell into a dish of soft soap, and in cleaning it with ashes and a sponge, the holes became stopped.

"It won't muse no more," said Flyaway, in sad surprise, blowing into the keys in vain. Ruth loved the little child too well to say she was glad of it.

Flyaway's next dash was into the sink cupboard, where she found a wooden bowl of sand. This she dragged out, and filling her "nipperkin" with water, carried them both to Ruth, saying, in her sweet, pleading way,—

"If you please, Ruthie, will you tell how God does when he takes the 'little drops of water and little grains of sand,' and makes 'the mighty oshum' with um, 'and the pleasant land'?"

Ruthie had no answer but a kiss and a smile.

"There, away with you into the nursery, both of you. I know Polly Whiting is lonesome without you."

Off went the children, Flyaway "with a heart for any fate," but Dotty still oppressed by the shadow of the ten-cent piece.

"If I don't give it to Prudy, will I be dishonest? Will I be as bad as Jennie Vance?"

When they entered the nursery, Miss Polly was standing before the mirror, arranging her black cap, and weaving into her collar a square black breast-pin, which aunt Louise said looked like a gravestone. Flyaway peeped in too, placing her smooth pink cheek beside Miss Polly's wrinkled one.

"I don't look alike, Miss Polly," said she; "and you don't look alike too."

Certainly not; no more alike than a blush-rose bud and a dried apple.

"What makes the red go out of folks' cheeks when they grow old, and the wrinkles crease in, like the pork in baked beans?" queried Dotty.

"I couldn't tell you," replied the good lady, giving a pat to her cap, and settling the bows carefully; "but if you had asked how I happened to grow old before my time, I should say I'd had such a hard chance through life, and trouble always leaves its mark."

"Does it? O, dear! I have trouble,—ever so much; will it quirk my face all up, like yours?"

"You have trouble, Dotty Parlin? Haven't you found out yet that the lines have fallen to you in pleasant places?"

"I don't know what you mean by lines," said Dotty, thinking of fish-hooks; "but when it rains, and folks want me to do things that are real hard, then why, I'm blue, now truly."

"Then we're blue, now truly," added Flyaway by way of finish.

"What would you do, children, if you were driven about, as I used to be, from post to pillar, with no mother to care for you?"

"If I hadn't no mamma, I could go barefoot, like a dog," said Flyaway, brightening with the new idea; "I could paddle in the water too, and eat pepnits."

"O, child! But what if you had neither father nor mother?"

"Then," said Flyaway coolly, "I should go to some house where there was a father'n mother."

"Why, you little heartless thing! But that is always the way with children; their parents set their lives by them, but not a 'thank you' do they get for their love! Try a pinch," continued she, offering her snuff-box to the little folks, who both declined. This Polly thought was strange. They must like snuff if they followed the natural bent of their noses.

"Yes, Katie, as I was saying, you little know how your mother loves you."

"Yes um, I do. She loves me more 'n the river, and the sky, and the bridge. My papa loves me too, only but he don't say nuffin' 'bout it."

"Yes, yes; just so," said Miss Polly, who talked to the simplest infants just as she did to grown people. "One of these days you will look back, and see how happy you are now, and be sorry you didn't prize your parents while you had them."

Flyaway rested her rosy cheek on Polly's knee, and watched the gray knitting-work as it came out of the basket. She did not understand the sad woman's words, but was attracted by her loving nature, and liked to sit near her, a minute at a time, and have her hair stroked.

"There, now," said Dotty, "you are knitting, Miss Polly; and it's so lonesome all round the house, with mother not coming till to-morrow, that I should think you might tell—well, tell an anecdote."

"I don't know where to begin, or what to say," replied Polly, falling into deep thought.

"I just believe she does sigh at the end of every needle," mused Dotty; "I'm going to keep 'count. That's once."

"Please, Miss Polly, tell a nanny-goat," said Flyaway, dancing around the room. "Please, Miss Polly, and I'll kiss you a pretty little kiss."

"Twice," whispered Dotty.

"Well, I'll tell you something that will pass for an anecdote, on condition that you call me aunt Polly; that name warms my heart a great deal better than Miss Polly."

"Three!" said Dotty aloud. "We will, honestly, if we can think of it, aunt Polly.—Four."

"Le'me gwout for the sidders, first," said busy Flyaway.

"There, aunt Polly, you forgot it that time! You sprang up quick to shut the door, and forgot it."

"Forgot what?"

"You didn't sigh at the end of your needle."

"Why, Dotty, how you do talk! Any one would suppose, by that, I was in the habit of sighing! I have a stitch in my side, child, and it makes me draw a long breath now and then; that's all."

Flyaway was back again,

"With step-step light, and tip-tap slight

Against the door."

"Come in," said Dotty, "and see if you can keep still two whole minutes; but I know you can't."

Miss Polly let her work fall in her lap, and drew up the left sleeve of her black alpaca dress. "Do you see that scar, children?"

It was just below the elbow,—an irregular, purple mark, about the size of a new cent.

"Why, Miss—why, aunt Polly!"

"I've got one on me too," said Flyaway, pulling at her apron sleeve; "Hollis did it with the tongs."

"It can't be; not a scar like mine."

"Bigger 'n' larger 'n' yours; only but I can't find it," said Flyaway, carefully twisting around her dainty white arm, which Polly kissed, and said was as sweet as a peach. "Bigger 'n' larger 'n' yours. Where's it gone to? O, I feegot—'twas on my sleeve, and I never put it on to-day."

"You're a droll child, not to know the difference between scars and dirt! When I was almost as young and quite as innocent, that wicked little boy bit me, and I shall carry the marks of his teeth to my grave." With another lingering glance at the purple mark, Polly drew down her sleeve, sighed, and began to knit again.

"Was it the woman's child that made you dig, that you told about last summer?"

"Yes; I was a bound girl."

"Bound to what?" Dotty was trying to drown the remembrance of Prudy's ten cents; so she wished to keep Miss Polly talking.

"Bound to Mrs. Potter till I was eighteen years old. Her husband kept public house. They made a perfect slave of me. When I was twelve years old I had to milk three cows, besides spinning my day's work on the flax-wheel. And very often all I had for supper was brown bread and skim milk. I didn't have any grandfather's house to go to, with a seat in the trees, and a boat on the water, and a swing, and a summer house, and a crocky-set (croquet set). Not I!"

Flyaway was cutting paper dolls with all speed, but her sweet little face was drawn into curves of pity.

"Too bad! Naughty folks to give you skilmick."

"I had to scour all the knives too. I did it by drawing them back and forth into a sand-bank back of the house. This Isaac I speak of was a lazy boy, and very unkind to me; but his mother wouldn't hear a word against him. One day I brushed a traveller's coat, and got a silver quarter for my trouble. I thought everything of that quarter. I had never had so much money before in my life. I had half a mind to put it in the Savings Bank; 'and who knows,' thought I, 'but I can add more to it, one of these days, and buy my time.'"

"Why, Miss Polly, I didn't know you could buy time!"

"But you knew you could throw it away, I suppose," said Polly, with a sad smile. "What I mean is this: I wanted to pay Mrs. Potter some money, so I could go free before I was eighteen."

"Then you would be unbound, aunt Polly."

"Yes; but one day Isaac found my money,—I kept it in an old tobacco-box,—and, just to hector me, he kept tossing it up in the air, till all of a sudden it fell through a crack in the floor; and that was the last I saw of it."

"HERE HE IS!"

"What a naughty, careless boy!"

After Dotty had said this, she blushed.

"Naughty, careless boy!" echoed Flyaway. "Here he is!" holding up a paper doll shaped very much like a whale, with the fin divided for legs, the ears of a cat, and the arms of a windmill. "Here he is!"

"He didn't look much like that," said Polly, laughing. "He had plenty of money of his own, and I tried to make him give me back a quarter; but do you believe he wouldn't, not even a ninepence? And when I teased him, that was the time he bit my arm."

"He oughtn't to bitted your arm, course, indeed not!"

"But, aunt Polly," faltered Dotty, whose efforts to forget the ten-cent piece had proved worse than useless, "but it didn't do Isaac any good to lose your money down a crack."

"No, it was sheer mischief."

"And if it doesn't do folks any good to lose things, you know, why, what's the use—to—to—go and get his own money to pay it back with?—Isaac I mean."

"What do you say, Dotty Parlin? You, a child that goes to Sabbath school! Don't you know it is a sin to steal a pin? And if we lose or injure other people's things, and don't make it up to them, we're as good as thieves."

"As good?"

"As bad, then."

"But s'posin'—s'posin' folks lose things when they don't toss 'em up in the air, and don't mean to,—the wind, you know, or a kind of an accident, Miss Polly,—"

"Well?"

"And s'posin' I didn't have any more money 'n I wanted myself, and Prudy had the most—H'm—"

"Well?"

"Then it isn't as bad as thieves; now is it? She's got the most. Prudy's older 'n I am—"

"Honesty is honesty," said Miss Polly, firmly, "in young or old. If you've lost your sister's money, you must make it up to her."

"O, must I, Miss Polly? Such a tinty-tonty mite of money as I've got,—only sixty-five cents."

"Honesty is honesty," repeated Miss Polly, "in rich or poor."

"Dear me! will my mother say so, too?"

"Your mother is on the right side, Dotty. The Bible tells us to 'deal justly.' There's nothing said there about excusing poor folks."

"O, dear! do you s'pose the Bible expects me to pay Prudy Parlin ten cents, when it just blew out of my hands, and didn't do me a speck of good?"

"Why, Dotty, you surprise me! Any one would think you were brought up a heathen! If you were a small child I could understand it."

"I knew I should have to do it," moaned Dotty.

"I advise you to lose no time about it, then; that is the cause of your blues, I guess. We can't be happy out of the line of our duty," sighed Miss Polly, who regarded herself as a pattern of cheerfulness.

"I'll tell you what I'm going to do," said Dotty, resolutely; "I'm going right off to pay that money to Prudy, and then I'll be in the line of my duty."

CHAPTER XII.

FULL NIPPERKIN.

Prudy scorned to take the ten cents. "Did you think your 'middle-aged' sister would do such a thing, when she has more money than you have, Dotty Dimple? If you're only sorry, that's all I ask. I didn't like to have you laugh, as if you didn't care."

"But, Prudy, I want to be honest."

"And so you have been, dear child," said grandma Parlin, with an approving smile. "If Prudy chooses now to give you the money, receive it as a present, and say, 'Thank you.'"

"O, thank you, Prudy Parlin, over and over, and up to the moon," cried Dotty, throwing her arms around her kind sister's neck. "I'll never lose anything of yours again; no, never, never!"

This lesson was laid away on a shelf in Dotty's memory. Close beside it was another lesson, still more wholesome.

"Dotty Dimple isn't the best girl that ever lived. She had to be talked to and talked to, before she was willing to do right. She isn't any better than Jennie Vance, after all. Why did she pray that naughty prayer, just to make Jennie feel bad? God must have thought it was very strange!"

Grandma saw that Dotty's "blues" were dissolving like a morning mist; still she knew the child was in need of patchwork, and told her so.

"Let us all take our work," said she, "and sit together in the nursery, so we may forget the dull weather."

Grace brought her piqué apron down stairs to make, Susy her tatting, Prudy a handkerchief, Dotty a square of patchwork, while Flyaway danced about for a needle and thread.

"What a happy group!" said Mrs. Clifford, looking up from her sewing. She had forgotten Polly Whiting, who was mournfully toeing off a sock for Horace, while he sat on the floor, at her feet, mending her double-covered basket.

"Why, Katie, darling," said Grace, "what are you doing with that beautiful ribbon?"

"Aunt Louise said I might make a bag, Gracie—"

"Seems to me aunt Louise lets you do everything; I shouldn't want you to spoil that ribbon."

"They shan't bother my little Topknot," said Horace, with a sweep of his thumb. "She is going to have all my clothes to make bags of, when she grows up."

Flyaway, who knew she had a good right to the ribbon, pressed her eyelids together slowly.

"If I's Gracie," said she, severely, "I'd make aprons; if I's mamma I'd sew dresses; if I's Flywer, I'd do just's I want to."

And then she went on sewing; without any thimble.

"Girls, have you guessed yet why a wheelbarrow is like a potato?"

"No, Horace; why is it?"

"O, I was in hopes you could tell. I don't know, I am sure. It is as much as I can do to make up a conundrum, without finding out the answer."

The children laughed at this, but none of them so loud as Flyaway, who thought her brother the wisest, wittiest, and noblest specimen of boyhood that ever lived.

"How our needles do fly!" said Dotty, merrily.

She was a neat and swift little seamstress, even superior to Prudy.

"See," said Flyaway to Horace; "I work faster 'n my mamma, 'cause she's got a big dress to work on: of course she can't sew so quick as I can on a little bag."

"Prudy can sew better and faster than I can," said Dotty, with a sudden gush of humility.

"Why, Dotty Dimple, I don't think so," returned Prudy, quite surprised.

"Neither do I," said aunt Maria; "I am afraid our little Dotty is hardly sincere."

Dotty's head drooped a little. "I know it, auntie; I do sew the nicest; but I was afraid it wouldn't be polite if I told it just as it was, and Prudy so good to me, too."

"If she is good, is that any reason why you should tell her a wrong story?" remarked the plain-spoken Susy, giving a twitch to her tatting-thread.

"Children," said Mrs. Clifford, laughing, "do you remember those hideous green goggles I wore a year ago?"

"O, yes 'm," replied Grace; "they made your eyes stick out so! Why, you looked like a frog, ma', more than anything else."

"Well, a certain lady of my acquaintance was so polite as to tell me my goggles were very becoming."

"O, ma, who could it have been?"

"I prefer not to give you her name. I appreciated her kind wish to please me, but I could not think her sincere."

"O, Susy," said Grace, "if you could have seen those goggles! A little basket for each eye, made of green wire, like a fly cover! Ma, did you ever believe a word that lady said afterwards?"

"Flatterers are not generally to be trusted," replied Mrs. Clifford. "Flyaway, that is the fourth needle you have lost."

Here was another lesson for Dotty's memory-shelf. "I must not say things that are not true, just to be polite. It is flattering and wicked; and besides that, people always know better."

It was a quiet, busy, cheerful day. Dotty forgot to complain of the weather. Just before supper Flyaway jumped down from her grandpapa's knee, where she had been talking to him through his "conversation-tube," and ran to the window.

"Why, 'tisn't raining," cried she; "true's I'm walking on this floor 'tisn't raining!"

Dotty clapped her hands, and watched the sun coming out like pure gold, and turning the dark clouds into silver.

"We were patient and willing for it to rain," said she; "but of course that wasn't why it cleared off."

And it wasn't why Flyaway lost her thumb-nail, either. She lost that—or half of it—in the crack of the door. The poor little thumb was very painful, and had to be put in a cot.

"It wearies me," said Flyaway; "it makes me afraid I shan't ever have a nail on there again."

Her mother assured her she would. The same God who calls up the little blades of grass out of the ground could make a finger-nail grow.

"Will He?" said Flyaway, smiling through tears; "but 'haps He'll forget how it looks. Musn't I save a piece of my nail, mamma, and lay it up on the shelf, so He can see it, and make the other one like it?"

Mrs. Clifford put the nail in her jewel-box, and I dare say it may be there to this day.

Just as Flyaway, in her nightie, was having a frolic with Grace, there was a sound of wheels. The stage, which Horace called the "Oriole" because it had a yellow breast, was rolling into the yard.

"It's my mother—my mother," cried the three Parlins together.

Yes, and who was that little girl getting down just after her? Her hat covered her eyes. "It isn't Tate Penny!" Why, to be sure it was! There was her dimpled chin; and if that wasn't proof enough, there was the wart on her thumb!

To think such a glorious thing as this could happen to Dotty! and she not the best girl in the world either! A visit from her bosom friend! "Aunt 'Ria, do you understand? Aunt Louise? Gracie? This is Tate Penny!"

"Who asked her to come? How did she happen to be with mamma, the same day, in the same cars?"

Well, grandma Parlin invited her to come. "When one lives in an India-rubber house," she said, "a few people more or less make no difference at all. She wished Dotty's 'nipperkin' of happiness to be full for once."

And it was: it ran over. There were joyful days for the next fortnight. I could never draw the picture of them with my pen, even if I had the paper left to put it on. They kept house under the trees; they baked their food in a brick oven Horace made; they gave a party; they had boat rides; they had swings; they never went into the house unless it rained; they were never cross to one another, or rude to Jennie Vance; it was like living in fairy-land.

It was a glorious summer. I almost wish it had not come to an end; though, in that case, I suppose I should never have stopped telling about it. By and by vacation was over, and Tate went off in the same stage with the Parlins. You could never guess what she and Dotty each put so carefully into their bosoms, to keep "forever." It was a splinter of the dear old barn where they had had such good times jumping!

Three weeks afterwards the "Oriole" drove up to grandpapa Parlin's again, and this time for the Cliffords. Flyaway danced into it like a piece of thistle-down. Everybody threw good-by kisses, and the stage rattled away.

And after that, dears, as Flyaway will say to her grandchildren, "things went into a mist." And this is all I have to tell you about the Parlins, the Cliffords, and the Willowbrook home.

THE END.